The Norwood Author

Arthur Conan Doyle and the Norwood Years
(1891 - 1894)

Alistair Duncan

D1248718

First edition published in 2010
© Copyright 2010
Alistair Duncan

The right of Alistair Duncan to be identified as the author of this
work has been asserted by him in accordance with the Copyright,
Designs and Patents Act 1998.

Although every effort has been made to ensure the accuracy of
the information contained in this book, as of the date of
publication, nothing herein should be construed as giving advice.
The opinions expressed herein are those of the author and not of
MX Publishing.

Paperback ISBN 9781904312697
Published in the UK by MX Publishing
335 Princess Park Manor, Royal Drive, London, N11 3GX
www.mx-publishing.co.uk

This book is dedicated to Andy Collins.

1951 - 2009

A lover of fine wine, fine food, fine ale and fast horses whose life was cut short by cancer.

Donations welcome to any cancer charity or directly to The Hospice of St Francis at Berkhamsted where he occasionally stayed.

Contents

About the author

Alistair Duncan is an I.T. Consultant and Sherlock Holmes enthusiast. Since the early 1980s he has been a fan of the Great Detective. He is a member of the Sherlock Holmes Society of London, the Conan Doyle (Crowborough) Establishment and The Sydney Passengers.

He lives with his wife in South London.

ii

Also by the same author

Eliminate the Impossible

Close to Holmes

iv

Acknowledgements

I extend my principal thanks to Brian Pugh without whose recent book *A Chronology of the Life of Sir Arthur Conan Doyle* I would have found many dates rather elusive. Except where stated otherwise, event dates have been sourced from Brian's book. Hence my thanks also go to all those authors from whose work Brian sourced the dates originally (please see the bibliography).

Equal thanks are due to the staff of the Local Studies Department of Croydon Library (especially Christine Corner and Chris Bennett) who answered an untold number of e-mails and tolerated me monopolising the microfilm reader for hours at a time as I poured through issues of *The Norwood News* and other newspapers seeking cricket results and other Doylean facts.

In addition, I would like to formally acknowledge the following for their support, encouragement and assistance:

Bill Barnes (President of the Sydney Passengers), Catherine Cooke (Sherlock Holmes Collection: Marylebone Library, Westminster Libraries), Phil Cornell (Vice-President of the

Sydney Passengers), John Coulter (Local Studies Department, Lewisham Library), Dr. Robin Darwall-Smith (Archivist - University College, Oxford), Steve Duke (Sydney Passengers), John Hickman (South Norwood Historian), Paul Howarth (Curator - The Gilbert & Sullivan Archive), Roger Johnson (Sherlock Holmes Society of London), Meirian Jump (Archives Assistant - Oxford University Archives), Helen F. Keen (Heritage Public Services - Surrey History Centre), Jeremy Nicholas (President of the Jerome K. Jerome Society), Tom Ruffles (Society for Psychical Research), Jerry Savage (Reference & Local History Librarian - Upper Norwood Joint Library), Paul Spiring (Doylean Author).

Many of the pictures reproduced within these pages are now in the public domain but those from collections such as those of Brian Pugh, Croydon Library and the Society for Psychical Research may not be reproduced without permission from those individuals or organisations.

Efforts have been made to identify material still under copyright and seek permission for use. If I have overlooked any item the copyright holder is asked to contact the publisher so that the matter can be rectified in any future edition of this book.

Foreword

✦

For Arthur Conan Doyle, the years 1891-1894 were a series of thrilling highs and some quite devastating lows. These high points included the momentous and joyful decision to give up his stagnating medical career and concentrate on writing for a living (something he described as "one of the great moments of exultation of my life"); the birth of his second child (and first son); widespread literary success and the writing of some of his most interesting work – *The Stark Munro Letters*, *The Refugees*, *The Great Shadow*, around a third of the Sherlock Holmes stories and "my first venture in the drama", the successful *A Straggler of '15*. The low points were family tragedies – his wife being diagnosed with an incurable disease and given only a few months to live; to be followed soon after by the death of his father. During this period Conan Doyle lived a suburban life in South Norwood, London and Alistair Duncan has delved into the minutiae of this time to give us the details of Conan Doyle's involvement in his local environs, particularly in three enduring aspects of his life – the sporting, the literary and the scientific.

This phase of Conan Doyle's life was also the latter part of his introduction to the literary life of London. As a young and rising author he had mixed with other young writers also in the process of making a name for themselves – Rudyard Kipling, H. G. Wells and his contemporaries James Barrie, George Bernard Shaw and Jerome K. Jerome. His interest in psychic phenomena and their scientific investigation had also strengthened sufficiently by this time for him to join the Society for Psychical Research, an association he maintained for the next 36 years.

My connection with Alistair Duncan started at the beginning of 2009 when he joined the Sherlock Holmes society of which I am currently the president. I had bought a copy of his previous book, *Close to Holmes*, was impressed with it and wrote a review, including some minor quibbles, for the journal of that society. Alistair saw the review, thought I'd done a reasonable job, graciously accepted my criticisms and later enquired if I'd like to do the foreword for his next effort. I was honoured to be asked to contribute.

The title of this book, *The Norwood Author*, could well relate to Alistair himself. Living in South Norwood, like Conan Doyle, and having now written three books on associated subjects, he is well placed to provide us with the detailed history of these important years in Conan Doyle's life. Alistair also has more than just a domiciliary connection to the area – he was instrumental in greatly improving the community's recognition of the famous author by having a local public house mount a permanent display on Conan Doyle, with an immediate positive effect. This book was not written as a biography, although it contains much biographical material. Its strength lies in fleshing out an interesting and dramatic period in Arthur Conan Doyle's life and covers detail that wide-ranging biographies don't necessarily delve into.

In mid 1893 Conan Doyle and his wife travelled to Switzerland on a lecture visit. Whilst there he discovered the Reichenbach Falls and hit upon it as the perfect setting for the demise of Sherlock Holmes, something that had been exercising his mind for quite some time. Not long after returning home, Louise Conan Doyle was diagnosed with what we now know as tuberculosis and this energised Conan Doyle into action to move to a better climate for her. Holmes's end was another (then) high point for Conan Doyle; quite the opposite, however, for the reading public and the magazine publishers. The story of Holmes's "death" was published simultaneously in the UK and USA in December 1893 and by that time Conan Doyle had effectively also said goodbye to South Norwood.

Arthur Conan Doyle was a complex and deeply interesting character. May there long be writers around such as Alistair Duncan to explore him.

Bill Barnes
'Captain' (president), The Sydney Passengers

x

Introduction

It is reasonably fair to say that Sir Arthur Conan Doyle is one of the most written about men in the world. The fact that he merits this level of attention comes down primarily to two things - his creation of Sherlock Holmes and his much mocked interest in spiritualism.

In general the biographies that exist focus on his entire life and, as a result, certain periods get more attention than others. This is either because they were brief or that the biographer's focus was not served by spending too much time on them. One such period is 1891 - 1894 when Conan Doyle was a resident of South Norwood in present day South East London.

The relationship between Conan Doyle and South Norwood is a strange one. Although he lived in the area for some years he appears to have left little lasting impression. This is presumably down to the fact that for a lot of the time that he occupied 12 Tennison Road he was away on business either abroad or elsewhere in the United Kingdom.

Other biographies, when covering this period of Conan Doyle's life, tend to limit themselves to talking about family events and his literary output. On the family front, his first son was born, his father died and his first wife was diagnosed with consumption (tuberculosis). From a literary standpoint, much of his best work (not just Sherlock Holmes) was either written or published during this period.

What has not been covered to any significant extent is Conan Doyle's involvement in local life. His membership of the Norwood Cricket Club and the Upper Norwood Literary and Scientific Society are the two most obvious examples of this local activity and are areas that shall be touched upon within these pages.

The biggest problem for any author, when writing about Arthur Conan Doyle, is that it is virtually impossible to avoid mentioning people or events that have been discussed in earlier works. I hope that the reader will be patient where this occurs and I also hope that the lesser known events detailed herein will compensate.

Alistair Duncan, London 2010

1891

Arrival

On June 25th 1891 Dr. Arthur Conan Doyle moved into his house at 12 Tennison Road, South Norwood[1]. The pressing question is how he came to move to the area at all.

A glance at existing biographies and chronologies reveals that the first half of 1891 was an especially busy time for Conan Doyle. The year opened with him leaving his Portsmouth medical practice and heading to Vienna to learn about the latest advances in ophthalmic medicine. When he found that his grasp of German was insufficient to fully absorb these new ideas he headed back to England via Italy and France. By the end of March he was living in London at Montague Place, just north of the British Museum, and attempting to establish himself as an eye specialist at 2 Upper Wimpole Street close to Harley Street.

It is widely stated, but not universally accepted, that not one patient troubled him in his new practice and this unwanted free

---

[1] *Conan Doyle* by Hesketh Pearson (Chapter 6).

time provided the perfect opportunity to write[2]. April was mostly taken up as a result with writing the early Sherlock Holmes short stories and these were gradually dispatched to his agent A.P. Watt who sent them on to *The Strand* magazine and handled, what Conan Doyle described as, 'all the hateful bargaining...' This flurry of writing was interrupted in May by a severe bout of influenza which confined Conan Doyle to his bed for three weeks[3]. It was during this enforced rest that he took stock of his life which, in his medical opinion, he came quite close to losing and made his momentous decision to abandon medicine and become a full-time author. The period between the end of his illness and his move to South Norwood was little more than three to four weeks.

It is impressive therefore that in those few weeks he managed to cut short his Upper Wimpole Street lease, contact (or, as he put it, 'haunt') house-agents, visit suggested properties, decide on South Norwood and relocate there. It was certainly a timetable that would challenge anyone in England today.

---

[2] As revealed in *Arthur Conan Doyle: A Life in Letters*, Conan Doyle later contradicted himself on his workload. In an interview entitled *Celebrities at Home: Mr Arthur Conan Doyle in Tennison Road*, which appeared in the August 3rd 1892 issue of the magazine *World: A Journal for Men and Women*, Conan Doyle said that the demands of his practice were such that it was getting in the way of his writing and this was one of the reasons behind his decision to abandon medicine.

[3] In his autobiography, *Memories and Adventures,* Conan Doyle states that his illness and decision to abandon medicine took place in August 1891. This cannot be the case as his later Norwood cricket appearances make clear (see later).

But why did he target the Norwood area in particular? His autobiography makes plain that he was after a suburban property but Norwood was hardly the only suburb. It is a question that many biographers choose to ignore and, in the absence of hard evidence, it is difficult to blame them. In an effort to find an answer we are forced to enter the realms of conjecture but it is certainly possible that it had something to do with the fact that he was already familiar with the area[4]. He had visited the Crystal Palace in Upper Norwood when he was a boy and the fact that the Norwood area made an impression on him is beyond debate as it was the scene of the crime in his second Sherlock Holmes story *The Sign of Four*.

It can therefore be argued that if the area held sufficient interest for him to set a story there it could have easily been an equally attractive prospect to live there. Ultimately however he ended up living not in Upper Norwood but at 12 Tennison Road, South Norwood[5]. This may have been down to cost or not being

---

[4] Conan Doyle's letters, as revealed in *A Life in Letters*, do not assist us in our search for a reason. The first letter written from South Norwood is from September 1891 and the tone of the letter suggests that he has been resident for some period of time (i.e. there is no description of the move itself). This backs up the idea that he moved to the area earlier than he himself suggested in his autobiography.

[5] A study of the 1891 census, which was taken in April when Conan Doyle was still at Montague Place, reveals that the residents of 12 Tennison Road at that time were a Mr Thomas Bulling and his wife Harriett. The couple, who were in their seventies, were presumably finding the running of such a large house difficult (no one else was listed as living there - not even domestic staff) and were possibly moving to a smaller house. It appears that the house was not vacated

able to find the right property (issues all too familiar to house hunters). However it is interesting to note that despite opting to live in South Norwood he would spend a lot of his time in the local area in or close to Upper Norwood[6].

His decision to move to the area and abandon medicine was not without risk as his writing career was not exactly firmly established. It was true that he had, by this time, been published many times and his story *The White Company* was being serialised in *The Cornhill Magazine* but the literary fame, fortune and security that Sherlock Holmes would bring were still in the future. Holmes's first two adventures[7] had not made much of an impact and *The Strand* magazine, which had only launched in January, was yet to publish the first of the new Holmes short

---

due to a death as neither of the Bullings appears in the death records for that year.

[6] The 1896 rate book for the Croydon borough reveals that most of the houses in Tennison Road, including number twelve, were tenanted. The owner in each case was listed simply as 'Mears'. This is almost certainly Joseph Mears who was a Hammersmith based builder responsible for a considerable number of London houses and other buildings. It is therefore likely, in line with common practice at the time, that the first tenant had purchased a long lease from Mears and then the remainder of this lease had been eventually sold to Conan Doyle (presumably by Thomas Bulling - see footnote 5). So Conan Doyle almost certainly did not own his house in South Norwood.

[7] *A Study in Scarlet* and *The Sign of Four*. Published in *Beeton's Christmas Annual* (1887) and *Lippincott's Monthly Magazine* (1890) respectively.

stories. Herbert Greenhough Smith and George Newnes, the editor and publisher respectively, received the first five manuscripts (starting with *A Scandal in Bohemia*) between April and May but were not to begin publishing them until July. This delay in publication may possibly have been, in part, caused by Conan Doyle's illness and the move to South Norwood. It is possible that Greenhough Smith did not wish to commence publication of the stories until he knew the sixth (and initially final) story, *The Man with the Twisted Lip*, was underway. In the end this was not sent by Conan Doyle to his agent until August. What seems certain is that Conan Doyle, Greenhough Smith and Newnes were unaware of the scale of the literary impact they were about to make.

*Crystal Palace c1890 - Conan Doyle visited the site as a boy when on holiday
from school*

12 Tennison Road in 1892 (taken from The Strand Magazine)

Herbert Greenhough Smith - Editor of The Strand (from August 1892 issue)

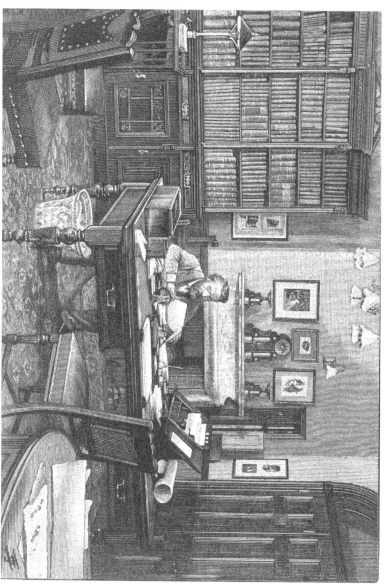

George Newnes - Publisher of The Strand (from August 1892 issue)

Early Days

The South Norwood of the 1890s, in common with its twenty-first century incarnation, attracted many people who worked in the City of London by virtue of its easy connection to London Bridge station via Norwood Junction. Of the railway stations across the three Norwoods (Lower[8], Upper and South) it was only from this station that it was possible to get express trains into town (a fact that Conan Doyle would make use of in his later, post-Norwood, Holmes story *The Norwood Builder*).

Unlike the modern version, it should be noted that, in Conan Doyle's time, South Norwood was in the county of Surrey and, whilst still seen as a London commuter suburb, would have, in all probability, lacked the London atmosphere that it has today[9]. It was therefore well placed to be popular with people who wanted all the attractions of a leafy suburb yet the easy access to town.

---

[8] The area is presently known as West Norwood.

[9] Since 1965, following the Local Government Act of 1963, South Norwood has been part of Greater London.

From a transport perspective Conan Doyle's occupancy of a house on Tennison Road had a distinct advantage. Not only was he some small distance apart from the main centre of South Norwood and its hustle and bustle but he was also equidistant from the two principal railway stations. Norwood Junction station was only a five to ten minute walk from his home and a similar walk in the opposite direction would bring him to Selhurst station[10]. This station ran frequent trains into London Victoria so he therefore had straightforward access to both the City and the West End. The latter was of course necessary for trips to the offices of George Newnes and Greenhough Smith at *The Strand*.

South Norwood was essentially a settlement of two halves with those halves being loosely defined by the railway line. The western side of the line was generally perceived to be the more affluent area where the middle classes lived. To the east was to be found the working class housing which tended to cater for the workers of employers such as Horris Parks Brickworks[11]. The

---

[10] It was just as well that Conan Doyle had easy access to Selhurst station. On May 2nd part of the Portland Road railway bridge, which carried trains that passed through Norwood Junction, collapsed when an express train passed over it. There was consequently severe disruption while it was repaired.

[11] The brickworks opened in the 1880s but was bought and renamed Handley's in 1910 (Source: Canning & Clyde Road Residents Association). Horris Parks himself was a close neighbour of Conan Doyle living at number 1 Tennison Road throughout the 1891 - 1894 period that Conan Doyle was at number 12. Another neighbour, who appears to have moved into the area during 1892, was one Augustus Charles Gifford. Gifford, who was a butcher who had moved to the

other local employer of note was Brock's Fireworks, founded in the early eighteenth century by John Brock. This company, which had relocated to South Norwood from Islington in the first half of the nineteenth century, had a long association with the nearby Crystal Palace and put on many free public displays[12].

Following his arrival Conan Doyle seems to have managed to keep a fairly low profile in so far as the press were concerned. Again this was in no small part down to the fact that he did not yet have the fame of Holmes to mark him out. He did however show that the swiftness with which he had moved to South Norwood was not a one off by moving equally swiftly to get involved in some community activities.

---

area from Essex, lived initially at number 18 but later moved to number 3 and was still resident when Conan Doyle moved out of the area. It is possible that the two men had an acquaintance and that Conan Doyle took his former neighbour's first two names and changed their order for the eponymous villain of his 1904 Holmes story *The Adventure of Charles Augustus Milverton*. However there are other candidates, some of whom have stronger claims.

[12] These continued intermittently until the destruction of Crystal Palace by fire in 1936.

The issue of *The Norwood News*[13] that was published on July 11th 1891 shows that Conan Doyle made his debut for the Norwood Cricket Club in an away game against nearby Addiscombe on June 30th [14]. Astonishingly this was a mere five days after he had moved into Tennison Road. It seems almost absurd that, in that small period of time, he could have moved to a new area, joined the local cricket team and demonstrated such skill as to cause the club to select him for the side. You would be forgiven for speculating that the Norwood Club had somehow been made aware of his Portsmouth record and had consequently welcomed him with open arms. However, a look at the papers quickly reveals that his swift deployment probably had little to do with his experience at Portsmouth but was more to do with the fact that one of the long-standing members of the team was suffering from intermittent ill-health and hence the club was occasionally struggling to field a full side. In other words, despite it not being very flattering, they welcomed anyone they could get.

---

[13] The paper, which had first been published on February 29th 1868, was a decidedly middle-class paper. This was demonstrated unambiguously in an article from July 8th 1893 which reported on some fireworks arranged in Croydon by the mayor. The article referred to the fact that many of the attendees 'were obvious [sic] of the class whose means would not permit them to see the fireworks at the Crystal Palace.'

[14] As stated earlier, the fact that Conan Doyle played in this game proves that he was not ill in central London and debating his future during August as stated in his autobiography.

However he made it into the team Conan Doyle's debut at Addiscombe was ultimately a successful one. When his turn came to bat he managed to score twenty-two runs before being bowled out. This number of runs made him the third highest scorer of his side coming behind A. Springett (who was run out) and L. de Montezuma. This alone would have proved to the club committee that the decision to field him was a good one. According to the same issue of *The Norwood News* he played again the following day (July 1st). This was a home game against Surrey Club and Ground but it was not to be another success - Conan Doyle was bowled out for nought.

One can only guess at what his wife Louise made of all this activity. With her husband immersing himself in his writing and local cricket she may have felt more than a twinge of déjà vu. Conan Doyle had, after all, managed to arrange things so that their honeymoon in Ireland had coincided with local cricket fixtures[15].

It is evident that the Norwood Cricket Club was highly impressed with its new recruit and one match in particular illustrates why. *The Norwood News* of July 18th 1891 carried details of a match against Norbury Park. Conan Doyle bowled out no less than five of the opposing team before going on to score thirty-two runs. This and his other impressive performances must have been the reason that he was an easy choice for the Norwood team's tour of Holland that summer which left England on August 15th and returned on the 26[th][16]. The

---

[15] *The Adventures of Arthur Conan Doyle* by Russell Miller.

[16] As stated earlier, Conan Doyle's first letter to his mother from South Norwood, as shown in *A Life in Letters*, comes after August when the

tour finished with a hard fought match at The Hague against a 'United Holland' side which the visitors won[17]. The tour was undoubtedly an experience of which Conan Doyle was particularly fond as a portrait of the team was later to be found hanging in his drawing room at Tennison Road[18].

Conan Doyle's rapid entry into the Norwood Cricket Club was not his only swift move. He must have also moved quite swiftly to join the Upper Norwood Literary and Scientific Society, an organisation that he was destined to rise rapidly through the ranks of as we shall see later. He had been a member of the equivalent society in Portsmouth so must have been glad that he could continue to take part in similar activities in Norwood. The society had only held its annual general meeting and elected its committee in mid-May[19] and therefore would have been very much occupied with the planning of lectures for the coming season which ran from the beginning of October to the end of March 1892. Regrettably, due to an absence of

---

tour would have taken place. It is possible that a letter was written, and later lost, which mentioned the tour but it would appear, from other letters, that his performance on the cricket pitch was not a subject of which he wrote during his Norwood years.

[17] *Conan Doyle* by Hesketh Pearson.

[18] This was reported by the journalist Harry How in his piece for *The Strand* of August 1892 entitled *A Day with Dr Conan Doyle*.

[19] This has been confirmed by the examination of issues of *The Norwood News*. In fact their schedule was very much the same as that of the Portsmouth society.

records, we cannot determine the exact time that he joined or the name of the person who proposed his membership. However it is probable that 1891 was the year his membership commenced.

The Chairman of the society at the time was the Reverend John Rice Byrne. Byrne, who was sixty-three, was a graduate of Oxford University and a resident of Upper Norwood[20]. He was not attached to a local parish and was described in census records as a 'Minister of Religion - without care of souls'. His day-to-day occupation was to act as Her Majesty's Assistant Inspector of schools[21]. As a Christian minister he was devout and conservative and his lack of tolerance in this area was destined to cause him and the society problems in the future.

The society secretary, with whom Conan Doyle must have communicated in order to join, was one Mr. H.B.M. Buchanan. According to the 1891 census we know that he earned his living as a private tutor and at the time of the census he was without a situation (described diplomatically in the census itself as being neither employer or employed). He held a B.A. (exact subject unknown) and was later to co-author a number of natural history books for children. We know little about him beyond this but he was undoubtedly a capable man as he was regularly voted onto

---

[20] According to the University of Oxford Archives, Byrne gained a second class honours in Literae Humaniores (or Classics) in 1850 from University College and was awarded his MA in 1854.

[21] His appointment to this position was announced in the *London Gazette* of August 8th 1862. Three years earlier, he was listed in *The Philanthropist, and Prison and Reformatory Gazette* as being on the committee of The Boys Home on Euston Road in St Pancras.

the society committee and was secretary for the entire time that Conan Doyle was resident in Norwood. That he wielded considerable influence is also clear as he was to virtually decide the leadership of the society some years later[22].

September was a quiet month for Conan Doyle. *A Case of Identity*, one of the dullest Sherlock Holmes stories, was published and his first cricket season came to an end. From his perspective it had certainly been a good season. He had arrived in the area, played a number of good domestic games and then toured in Holland with his new team. He had every reason to be proud of his achievements and the obvious faith that the Norwood club had shown in him.

The Norwood News, in its summing up of the 1891 season, did not paint such a good picture of Conan Doyle's contribution. It remarked that the Norwood team had done well 'notwithstanding the wet summer, and the consequent prevalence of difficult wickets.' It went on to mention that the team's success was due 'in great measure…to the infusion of some new blood.' Conan Doyle, who was not the only player to fall into this category, was described as having 'also greatly assisted both with bat and ball'. This was a positive assessment for sure but hardly a ringing endorsement.

Despite having not played a full season Conan Doyle still managed to come mid-table in the team batting averages and in fourteen innings had scored a total of one hundred and sixty-

---

[22] Buchanan did not limit himself to the UNLSS. According to the April 6th 1892 issue of *The Norwood News* he was also president of the Upper Norwood Debating Club. Another member of this club was a Mr A.C.R. Williams of whom we shall hear more later on.

seven runs. In the bowling averages he fared less well but he was destined to come on in leaps and bounds over the coming years[23].

October, in contrast to September, was busy. Conan Doyle's first season of Upper Norwood Literary and Scientific Society lectures commenced (although we do not know how many he attended), *The Boscombe Valley Mystery* was published and he made his application to become a member of the Reform Club, the first of three establishment clubs that he would eventually join. The process was long and he was not destined to hear the result for some eight months. He was proposed by James Payn, who had published *The White Company,* and seconded by Malcolm Morris, a consultant surgeon at the Skin Department of

---

[23] As a great fan and player of cricket it is not unreasonable to speculate that Conan Doyle would have purchased the *Wisden Cricketers' Almanack.* This publication came out once each year and had begun in 1864. In 1889 it introduced an award for the cricketers of the year. This award was given to five players each year (with some exceptions) that had made a significant impact on the game in the English season. In 1891 one of the five recipients was a Henry Wood who played for Surrey. It is highly tempting to think that Conan Doyle stored this name away for later use in his Sherlock Holmes story *The Adventure of the Crooked Man* which was published in July 1893.

St Mary's Hospital in London[24]. On the 26th of the same month, the publisher Smith, Elder & Co released a three volume edition of *The White Company*. This was promptly advertised in the press with *The Times* of October 27th mentioning it in their regular column *Publications To-Day*.

Conan Doyle sent out complimentary copies of the book to several people, one of whom, Douglas Sladen, was secretary to The Authors' Club which Conan Doyle had joined at around the same time. The club had been co-founded by fellow author Walter Besant earlier that year as a sister society to The Society of Authors[25]. Strangely, at its inception, the club was without a permanent base and initially moved between a series of temporary locations[26]. It is certainly possible that Sladen's copy of the book could have been passed to Besant at some point for his perusal. Besant's opinion of the story, if he had one, is not known. Conan Doyle and Besant were to have irregular contact over the coming years but they do not appear to have been much more than acquaintances.

---

[24] *The Invisible Light - The Journal of The British Society for the History of Radiology 21st Birthday Year 1987-2008* is the source for Morris' exact position.

[25] *Arthur Conan Doyle: A Life in Letters* edited by Jon Lellenberg et al.

[26] *The Graphic* of February 27th 1892 stated that the club, which was still without a permanent base, would endeavour to be located 'as near that centre of the civilised world, Piccadilly Circus, as possible.' The society was only open to men who were British subjects or citizens of the United States.

*South Norwood High Street (c1902). This is the view Conan Doyle may well
have had (but minus the electric trams) when travelling from Tennison Road
towards Upper Norwood or the Cricket Ground
(Courtesy of Croydon Local Studies Library)*

Norwood Junction train station South Norwood early 1900s. Conan Doyle would have almost certainly used this station on a semi-regular basis to travel into the City. To the right you can see Trythall Estate Agents through whom Conan Doyle may have arranged the lease on his house.
(Courtesy of Croydon Local Studies Library)

In the last week of October an event took place which was destined to have a significant effect on Conan Doyle's life in Norwood. Walter Besant's sister-in-law, Annie Besant, was a leading member of the Theosophical movement[27]. This movement, which had strong Hindu influences, combined a variety of belief systems and had been founded in 1875 by Helena Petrovna Blavatsky who later went on to be involved with other organisations such as the Hermetic Order of the Golden Dawn.

Walter Besant (date unknown)

---

[27] She was later to become a member of the Fabian Society at the suggestion of, Conan Doyle's sparring partner, George Bernard Shaw.

Mrs. Besant had been giving a series of lectures on the movement and had given one in the Croydon Public Hall, at the request of the local Theosophical Lodge, as recently as mid-September. A sub-committee of the Upper Norwood Literary and Scientific Society, led, according to *The Norwood News*, by a Mr. C. Redshawe Williams, had been tasked with arranging several debates and, confident that she would draw a large crowd, invited her to give a speech and take questions on the same subject in Upper Norwood in the last week of October. The invitation was accepted.

When society Chairman Reverend Rice Byrne saw the arrangements he was less than happy. Immediately after the committee elections in May he and some committee members had focused their attention on arranging the society's lecture schedule and had set up the sub-committee, under Redshawe Williams, to arrange the debates. The distinction between what was considered a lecture and what was considered a debate seems to have been somewhat flexible as both allowed question and answer sessions. However the convention appears to have been that in a debate no one person was expected to dominate the proceedings[28].

Byrne had taken absolutely no interest in the workings of the sub-committee after it had been set up and was later to state in a letter that when he saw the list of four speakers chosen to open the debates that year he had noted that he had 'no sort of sympathy...' with three of them. When it came to Annie Besant

---

[28] *The Norwood News* does not appear to have been entirely sure of the distinction either. In its coverage of the debate Annie Besant is referred to as the lecturer.

this was a huge understatement. Her estranged husband, Walter Besant's brother Frank, was, like Byrne, a clergyman with very conservative views. So conservative was he that when Annie Besant had begun to question her faith he had expelled her from the house and initiated the process of legal separation. Byrne would therefore have undoubtedly been pre-disposed to side with his fellow minister.

Mrs. Besant had gone on to fully reject Christianity and had become a member of the Secular Society - both moves unlikely to find much favour with a man like Byrne. The final straw, from his perspective, would have been that Mrs Besant had written a book called *The Law of Population: Its Consequences and Its Bearing Upon Human Conduct and Morals* which advocated birth-control and had been denounced by *The Times* as 'an indecent, lewd, filthy, bawdy and obscene book'. It is safe to say that it would have been extremely difficult to have found a person more likely than Annie Besant to offend the Reverend John Rice Byrne.

Despite his obvious hostility Byrne elected to attend Annie Besant's debate. Why he did this is not known for certain but it is quite possible that he feared that he would be seen as endorsing her appearance unless he made some show of opposition.

Grange Road, Thornton Heath (2009). According to census records, Reverend John Rice Byrne lived here up until his death.

The debate and his subsequent conduct were reported in *The Norwood News* of October 31st and dominated the paper's letters page for several weeks afterwards. Interestingly, the Theosophical movement was one that Conan Doyle himself had been interested in when he had first started to take an interest in psychic matters but he had later rejected it[29]. Given this rejection it is unlikely that he attended the debate but even if he had it is doubtful whether he would have realised the effect that it was to have on his life.

At the debate, which took place at the Royal Crystal Palace Hotel due to the larger than usual audience (some reports stated that at least five hundred people attended), Annie Besant stood and spoke about the origins and characteristics of the Theosophical movement. Despite the fact that it was supposed to be a debate, Redshawe Williams, who was in the chair, allowed her to speak for more than an hour. No doubt he had decided that she, as the invited speaker, deserved the most time. Whether Byrne agreed with this assessment at the time is open to speculation.

After Mrs. Besant had finished speaking Byrne got to his feet. He began by complimenting Mrs. Besant on her speech and stated that he 'could hardly find words to express his admiration...' of her skills as an orator. With the pleasantries over he then proceeded to criticise the Theosophical movement accusing it of being aristocratic and, unlike Christianity, inaccessible to the common man. In truth he probably cared little about its inaccessibility and his attack was more to do with how

---

[29] *The Adventures of Arthur Conan Doyle* by Russell Miller (Chapter 19).

Theosophy (and Mrs. Besant) offended his Christian principles. Mrs. Besant addressed his accusations (her exact response was not reported but witnesses claimed it was very impressive) and resumed her seat. Unsatisfied by her response, Byrne made an effort to resume his attack. He clearly had a lot more to say after his initial salvo and, as society chairman, he no doubt expected to be allowed the time to say it. In this he was to be severely disappointed.

Redshawe Williams, who realised that the length of time that he had permitted Mrs. Besant to speak had left little time for others, cut Byrne short after only a few minutes. Others were then allowed to speak before the debate was brought to a close. Byrne was incensed by what he clearly interpreted as a lack of respect for him and his position and upon arriving home he wrote a letter to *The Norwood News* in order to put his side of the debate.

He began with a thinly veiled attack on Redshawe Williams for his handling of the debate and stated that in his opinion the event could barely have been called a debate as most people had only been allowed a few minutes. He did however admit that, in this instance, Annie Besant had deserved a certain amount of preferential treatment as an invited guest. It seems reasonably clear that, in reality, he was not particularly concerned with how long Besant had spoken and was even less concerned with how long others had been allowed to speak. His only concern was about how he had been treated personally.

After this opening and after putting his case against the Theosophical movement he then stated that he was fully convinced that, in time, Mrs. Besant would realise that Christianity was the way forward and that she would eventually 're-enter the fold.' In this, as in so much else, he was to be mistaken.

Annie Besant (1847 - 1933)

Byrne closed his letter by stating that although he was the chairman of the society and, in that capacity, took full responsibility for the organisation of lectures he would accept no responsibility for the organisation of the debates as they had been organised by a sub-committee without his involvement. In other words he expected Redshawe Williams to take the brunt of any fall-out caused by the debates. The buck most definitely did not stop with him as far as he was concerned.

The Grape & Grain public house in Upper Norwood (2009). This occupies the site of the former Royal Crystal Palace Hotel where the Annie Besant debate took place and Reverend Rice Byrne sowed the seeds of his downfall in the UNLSS

With his letter finished and dispatched Byrne probably felt quite self-satisfied (and more than a little self-righteous). Little did he realise the schism that venting his anger was to cause in the society. A considerable number of society members had already been angered by his hostile conduct towards their guest at the meeting. When they read his letter they became even more so and, such was the level of dissatisfaction, some of them were prepared to move against him.

The first of these steps was taken by an unnamed member of the society who sent a copy of Byrne's letter to Annie Besant. The fact that they knew where to send it suggests that it could have been a member of the committee who had arranged her attendance in the first place. It is even conceivable that the sender was Redshawe Williams himself reacting to Byrne's criticism[30].

Mrs. Besant swiftly responded and her letter to her informant was printed in *The Norwood News* of November 7th. It was a very concise letter in which she limited her remarks to saying 'I do not think Mr. Rice Byrne's letter is worth answering; it reminds me of nothing so much as a very angry kitten, with arched back and swollen tail, spitting furiously at a supposed foe.'

Another contributor to the same issue, who went under the name 'One of the audience', expressed no surprise at the appearance of Byrne's 'very sore letter' and offered his thanks to Redshawe Williams for 'stopping a speech of the rev. gentleman

---

[30] We do at least know that the unidentified person was a man as Annie Besant's response began 'Dear Sir'.

which might have been going on now, and which the audience certainly didn't want to hear.' He or she closed by expressing the hope that Byrne would not attend future debates. Another contributor, who went under the name of 'Fiat Lux'[31], stated that Byrne's words and actions were not those which were expected from 'a gentleman holding his position.'

However, the most interesting response came from Redshawe Williams himself. His letter, which also appeared in the November 7th issue, was civil but barely hid his frustration with Byrne. He tackled Byrne's complaint about the length of time he had been allowed to speak with the simple statement 'There is such a thing as the selfishness of public speaking.' Then, after examining some of Byrne's criticisms of Theosophy (and stating that he did not personally subscribe to it), he closed by addressing Byrne's complaints with regards to all of the arranged debates and their topics.

His words were simple yet effective. 'As to the debates of the society, there is no rule in existence limiting the subjects for debate to those with which the chairman has sympathy. The range, if such a rule existed, would, it seems, be a very narrow one.'

Byrne, predictably, did not take this lying down and his response appeared in the November 14th issue. In it he attempted to take on all his opponents at once and dismissed most of the people against him by stating that no one 'except the gentleman' had attempted to tackle any of his criticisms of Theosophy. The 'gentleman' concerned was clearly Redshawe Williams. In Victorian terms, the gloves were well and truly off.

---

[31] The Latin for 'Let there be light'.

The same issue of the paper carried one of the few letters in support of Byrne. Its author, Henri Viard, was very much of the same opinion as Byrne and also criticised Redshawe Williams and all those whom he saw as backing Theosophy at the expense of Christianity. Williams' inevitable response in the following issue came close to being libellous. He suggested that Viard was nothing more than a mouthpiece for Byrne and ended as follows:

'To conclude, it would be very interesting to trace the connection between the letter of Mr. Henri Viard and the views of Mr. Rice Byrne, and well worthy of the attention of Sherlock Holmes, as Mr. Conan Doyle names his famous amateur detective.'

After these exchanges there were no more letters from either Williams or Byrne upon the subject. What is certain is that Byrne came off worse from this very public battle. He had nailed his colours to the mast with the hope of much support but instead had generated considerable opposition. It must have occurred to him then or soon after that he might struggle to remain head of the society when the next AGM was held. He had taken the significant step of publicly criticising a fellow committee member and as a result he must have known that one of them would have to go. The other members of the committee would also have been very aware of this and would no doubt have been examining their options[32].

Despite the slightly different depiction of his name in *The Norwood News* it appears that Mr C. Redshawe Williams was actually Mr Alfred Charles Redshawe Williams. A.C.R. Williams was a solicitor and was Conan Doyle's solicitor for

---

[32] Some of the letters can be seen in appendix B.

some time after he left South Norwood[33]. How he came to be Conan Doyle's solicitor is not known. It is conceivable that he could have been involved in the acquisition of the lease for 12 Tennison Road or that Conan Doyle came to know him after his admission to the UNLSS. If the former it could easily have been the case that Williams was responsible for proposing Conan Doyle's admittance to the society.

Another curious fact about Williams is that he was, like Conan Doyle, interested in psychic matters and had joined the Society for Psychical Research in February 1889 some four years before Conan Doyle. The various issues of the publication *Proceedings of the Society for Psychical Research* from 1889 onwards list him as a member (in the format - Williams, A.C. Redshawe) with the 1894 issue displaying his Upper Norwood address. These documents, which enable us to make the link between A.C.R. Williams, C. Redshawe Williams, Upper Norwood and the various *Norwood News* articles, also suggest that the reason for Conan Doyle continuing to make use of Williams' services after he left Norwood was as much to do with him being a fellow SPR member as it was to do with Williams' legal skills[34]. It is also reasonably certain that Williams'

---

[33] *Conan Doyle: The Man who created Sherlock Holmes* by Andrew Lycett.

[34] In the SPR literature Williams' address was sometimes given as Bedford Row WC. Presumably this was the address of his employer and it enables us to make the definite link between Williams the SPR member and Williams the solicitor as an Alfred Charles Redshawe Williams appears in copies of *The Law List* at the same address.

psychic/spiritualist interest was the motive behind the decision to invite Annie Besant to talk about Theosophy[35].

During November a number of reviews of *The White Company* had been published. They varied in opinion and Conan Doyle was ambivalent about them but he probably looked on them all more fondly after December 11th brought a decidedly negative review from the *Pall Mall Gazette.*

This review contained a list of charges that Conan Doyle must have found hard to stomach. The review opened by stating 'It is with sincere regret that we confess our inability to regard Mr. Conan Doyle's new romance as entirely successful.' This was easily the kindest of all the remarks. The reviewer stated that large sections of the story could have been removed and not missed and that the story 'is not ill-composed - it is uncomposed. It consists of a series of adventures with no more continuity or interdependence than that of beads on a string.' The last two most cutting remarks were to state that 'Our curiosity, even when it is awakened, is never sustained' and 'we have neither absorbing fiction nor trustworthy history.'

On December 19th *The Times* contained an interesting entry under its section *Publications To-Day*. This was the entry for a new edition of *A Study in Scarlet* published by Ward, Lock and

---

[35] Tom Ruffles of the SPR states that, despite his long standing membership, A.C.R. Williams was not active in the society as his name appears nowhere other than in their list of members. Not once did he merit a mention in the society journal or any other literature.

Bowden. This edition, which was advertised at a cost of 3s 6d, was a less than subtle attempt on the part of Conan Doyle's earlier publisher to cash in on the success of the Sherlock Holmes short stories. When Conan Doyle sent his debut Holmes story around various publishers in 1886 it had been rejected time and again before Ward, Lock and Co. had accepted it. Not only did they then proceed to suppress it for a year, stating uncharitably to its author that the market was presently 'flooded with cheap fiction', they had also refused his request for royalties. Instead Conan Doyle had been forced to settle for twenty-five pounds for the entire rights.

When the story, which formed part of *Beeton's Christmas Annual*, appeared in 1887 it sank pretty much without trace[36]. Conan Doyle then abandoned Sherlock Holmes until his commission for a new story came from *Lippincott's Magazine* in 1889. Evidently, despite their decidedly poor assessment of the story as 'cheap fiction', Ward, Lock and Co clearly saw that they could now make money off the back of Sherlock Holmes's new found popularity by releasing a new edition of Holmes's debut appearance.

In an astonishing display of cheek they approached Conan Doyle for a special introduction for this new edition. He did not need too long to ponder this suggestion. He gleefully wrote to his mother about his refusal to co-operate with the request and

---

[36] The magazine was not designed to be retained and, like magazines today, most copies were thrown away after a few weeks. As a result of this there are very few copies in existence today and few of these are in good condition. Such is the rarity of original copies of the annual that even facsimiles sell for quite large sums.

Ward, Lock and Bowden were forced to simply release the original work, with illustrations from George Hutchinson.

December also saw Conan Doyle's first biographical entry in *The Strand*. He featured as part of the long running segment *Portraits of celebrities at different times of their lives*. The article, which only occupied one page, consisted of four pictures of Conan Doyle from age four to thirty-two and some text which amounted to little more than a who's who entry. The extraordinarily concise article quickly detailed his medical training, arctic experiences and his eventual abandonment of medicine for literature but was most notable for the fact that it made no mention of his father or mother but instead mentioned his grandfather and uncles. Whether this was because *The Strand* did not consider his parents interesting enough or that they were skipping them, particularly his father, at Conan Doyle's request is not clear.

Norwood Cricket Ground (2009) The Pavilion can be seen on the right. The boats that can be seen are used by the sailing club which uses South Norwood Lake which is immediately behind the cricket field.

Vanity Fair drawing of James Payn, editor of The Cornhill from 1883 and publisher of Conan Doyle's The White Company

1892

Beyond the City

The January 2nd issue of *The Norwood News* saw the introduction of a new feature. Simply entitled *Short Stories* it featured a story called *Crazy Jane* written by the Reverend Sabine Baring-Gould (1834 - 1924). It is not clear whether Conan Doyle and Baring-Gould knew each other well but they did share a common acquaintance in George Bernard Shaw and both were to attend the funeral of Alfred Tennyson on October 12th that same year. This was destined not to be the only link between the Baring-Gould family and Conan Doyle. Reverend Baring-Gould's grandson William (1913 - 1967) became a notable Sherlock Holmes scholar producing, amongst other Sherlockian works, the famous *Annotated Sherlock Holmes* in 1967[37].

---

[37] He also produced *Sherlock Holmes of Baker Street - the Life of the World's First Consulting Detective*. This fictional biography showcased many of Baring-Gould's more outlandish ideas. Some of these found their way into Hollywood films such as the idea that Holmes was involved in the hunt for Jack the Ripper.

Rev. Sabine Baring-Gould from The Strand c1893

It was around this time that Conan Doyle became involved with *The Idler* magazine. The magazine was launched that very month by the author Robert Barr, who often wrote under the pseudonym Luke Sharp, and was co-edited by him and Jerome K. Jerome whose name was famous thanks to his 1889 book *Three Men in a Boat*. Conan Doyle wrote to his mother on

January 6th to report that he had met with Barr, Jerome and J.M. Barrie at a dinner[38]. This dinner almost certainly included a discussion about Conan Doyle contributing to the new magazine.

The discussions were clearly productive and three days later (the 9th) the *Pall Mall Gazette* of that date carried a report of an interview with Jerome discussing the new magazine. Jerome was clearly enthusiastic about the new venture. When asked if the magazine was going to be humorous he displayed his characteristic wit by replying 'Great Scott no...did you ever know a magazine that was going to be humorous, that wasn't deadly dull? We're just going to be as good, as didactic, and as instructive as we know how. We shall then, in all probability, succeed in being tolerably amusing.'

The interviewer, after securing details of the content of the debut issue proceeded to ask Jerome about future issues and contributors. Jerome listed a number of authors with whom the magazine had 'already entered into contracts with...' Among the names listed was Conan Doyle's.

In fact Jerome, by his own admission, had managed to sign a significant number of what he called 'the most expensive writers in the world...' He estimated that the magazine would need to sell one hundred thousand copies a month in order to avoid being a costly failure and stated that he was pleased that none of his personal friends were among the shareholders. Whether this was another example of his famous wit or not is open to interpretation. His interviewer clearly was not sure either stating 'I couldn't quite discover whether Mr. Jerome was trying to be seriously amusing or amusingly serious...'

---

[38] *Arthur Conan Doyle: A Life in Letters* edited by Jon Lellenberg et al.

There was no piece by Conan Doyle in the debut issue perhaps due to the time his contract was drawn up. James Payn however did contribute with a story entitled *Her First Smile* that also appeared in other magazines including *Tauchnitz Magazine*[39].

Conan Doyle's first contribution to *The Idler* was *De Profundis* which appeared in March[40]. This was followed by a further five contributions - *The Los Amigos Fiasco, The Case of Lady Sannox, The Doctors of Hoyland, Sweethearts* and *The Stark Munro Letters*. All of these stories appeared between 1892 and 1894. After this time Conan Doyle appears to have ceased contributing.

---

[39] This was managed by Christian von Tauchnitz whom Conan Doyle had met at a dinner party with Payn in October 1891.

[40] The date on each magazine was one month ahead. The debut issue which was published on January 15th was referred to as the February issue. Therefore Conan Doyle's contribution must have been in the April issue. *De Profundis* was later republished in 1919 in a collection entitled *The Great Keinplatz Experiment and Other Tales of Twilight and the Unseen*.

The Case of Lady Sannox.

By A. Conan Doyle.

Illustrations by the Misses Hammond.

THE relations between Douglas Stone and the notorious Lady Sannox were very well known both among the fashionable circles of which she was a brilliant member, and the scientific bodies which numbered him among their most illustrious *confrères*. There was naturally, therefore, a very widespread interest when it was announced one morning that the lady had absolutely and for ever taken the veil, and that the world would see her no more. When, at the very tail of this rumour, there came the assurance that the celebrated operating surgeon, the man of steel nerves, had been found in the morning by his valet, seated on one side of his bed, smiling pleasantly upon the universe, with both legs jammed into one side of his breeches,

" SMILING PLEASANTLY UPON THE UNIVERSE."

and his great brain about as valuable as a cup full of porridge, the matter was strong enough to give quite a little thrill of interest to folk who had never hoped that their jaded nerves were capable of such a sensation.

Douglas Stone in his prime was one of the most remarkable men in England. Indeed, he could hardly be said to have ever for he was but nine-and-thirty at the time of

The start of Conan Doyle's third Idler contribution (from the second 1893 omnibus edition)

Jerome K. Jerome - Co-editor of The Idler (c1890) Reproduced with the permission of the Jerome K. Jerome Society

Robert Barr (a.k.a. Luke Sharp) - Co-editor of The Idler with Conan Doyle outside 12 Tennison Road in 1894 (Courtesy of Phil Cornell)

The January 16th issue of *The Norwood News* carried (as did all the subsequent issues of 1892) an advert for the Anerley Arms Hotel. The owner, George Bastow, was clearly a sporting man (or a fan of sports) as his advert made it plain that his club room (along with its piano) was available to gentlemen with connections to sporting clubs. One of the sports mentioned was cricket and it is therefore perfectly possible that the room may have been used on occasion by the members of the Norwood Cricket Club (nothing to prove or disprove this has so far been discovered). It would have been a relatively short journey from the clubhouse on Avenue Road to nearby Anerley Road and from there to Ridsdale Road where the Anerley Arms Hotel was situated[41].

It is pure speculation but it is not necessarily unreasonable to suggest that a visit here by Conan Doyle, perhaps in connection with the club, eventually led to the hotel featuring in the Sherlock Holmes adventure *The Norwood Builder*[42]. From the perspective of the Sherlockian this pub is interesting as, with the exception of some all too modern features, the interior of the Anerley Arms is very much as it would have been in Conan Doyle's time.

---

[41] One of the many routes between the two locations would have taken the traveller along Maberley Road. It is tempting to speculate that this road lent its name to the Maberley family that later featured in the 1926 Sherlock Holmes story *The Adventure of The Three Gables*.

[42] This story was published in 1903 nearly ten years after Conan Doyle had moved away from South Norwood.

THE

ANERLEY ARMS HOTEL,

ANERLEY

(Five minutes from Crystal Palace).

A large and well-matured Stock of

Wines, Spirits, Cigars,

&c., &c.

All the best known and approved

BRANDS OF CHAMPAGNE

A LARGE CLUB ROOM,

With Piano, at the disposal of Gentlemen
having to transact business connected with
Cricket, Football, Rowing, Bicycle, or other
Clubs ; also Smoking Concerts.

George Frederick Bastow,

PROPRIETOR.

*Advert for the Anerley Arms Hotel from The Norwood News of January 16th
1892*

The Anerley Arms in 2009

The interior of the Anerley Arms today (2009)

March 5th saw the publication of *The Doings of Raffles Haw* by Cassell and Co. Limited. This was not the first time the story had seen the light of day. It had been published twice during 1891 firstly in the *Pittsburgh Commercial Gazette* of July 12th and serialised in *Answers* between December 1891 and February 1892. Strangely, over a month passed before *The Times* of April 8th 1892 saw fit to comment on the latest release of this story.

The article was less than complimentary. The journalist stated that 'we doubt whether the externals of Dr. Conan Doyle's book are not superior to it contents.' The final comment on the story was that 'the idea is thin and rather grotesque. Dr. Doyle can do better than this.' This served to illustrate how Conan

Doyle's treatment at the hands of the critics was often at its worst when concerning non-Holmes publications[43].

April 30th 1892 saw the publication of *The Engineer's Thumb* in the *Baltimore Weekly Sun*. In addition it also saw one of the earliest mentions of Conan Doyle in *The Norwood News* that was not connected to cricket. Although brief it was an entry that would probably have pleased him.

He had spent Easter visiting J.M. Barrie in his home town of Kirriemuir. This places the trip around the 15th to 17th (Good Friday and Easter Sunday respectively). The trip was a fishing holiday but, according to *The Norwood News*, it also provided Conan Dole with the opportunity to indulge another passion. Reference was made to Conan Doyle's photographic skills describing him as 'an amateur photographer of considerable dexterity...' and went on to mention the photographs of 'The Window in Thrums and of other picturesque bits in the old red town.' that Conan Doyle had secured while there. It is open to question whether the reporter had actually seen the photographs as there were only two weeks between the holiday and the publication of the paper. It seems probable that Conan Doyle just told the reporter what subjects he had shot. It is equally possible that the reporter's analysis of Conan Doyle's skill could have been based on earlier photographs. He had after all been taking photographs for a good ten years prior to this date[44].

---

[43] Conan Doyle agreed with the poor opinion of *Raffles Haw*. He later wrote in his autobiography that it was 'not a very notable achievement.'

[44] According to Brian Pugh, the earliest published photographs taken by Conan Doyle appeared in *Cormorants With A Camera* which was

As stated, this article would almost certainly have pleased Conan Doyle. It would have managed this by the simple fact that no mention was made of Sherlock Holmes and Conan Doyle was instead referred to as 'the author of "The White Company"...'. As he was already tiring of Holmes, an article that omitted his detective and referred to one of his favourite works would have very likely found favour with him.

---

published in *The British Journal of Photography* on the 14th and 21st of October 1881.

Congratulations Mr. President

It seems likely that some time prior to early May Conan Doyle was approached and asked whether he would be prepared to stand for president of the Upper Norwood Literary and Scientific Society[45]. Reverend John Rice Byrne's conduct in October of the previous year had not been forgotten and some people were no doubt hoping for a change of leadership.

Who made the approach is not known for certain but if it is true that, at this time, A.C. Redshawe Williams knew Conan Doyle well, either as his solicitor or through their mutual interest in psychic matters, it is possible that he approached him to sound him out about the leadership. If this was indeed the case, revenge would have undoubtedly played its part as Williams was no doubt still smarting at the earlier criticisms levelled at him by Reverend Rice Byrne in the letters pages of *The Norwood News*. However Rice Byrne's conduct may have simply been a

---

[45] Reverend Rice Byrne always referred to himself as 'Chairman' of the society. It is therefore possible that the term 'President' only came into use in 1892.

convenient excuse for attempting to bring about something that was already desired. We know that Williams was a member of the Society for Psychical Research. What is less well known is that the UNLSS Secretary H.B.M. Buchanan, although not a member himself, was also interested (or becoming interested) in psychic matters. It is conceivable that between them they desired to bring about a pro-SPR dominance of the UNLSS committee. If Conan Doyle was elected president almost all of the top positions (the exceptions being the treasurer and one of the vice-presidents) would be held by people with a strong interest in psychic matters.

Whether this was how (and why) the approach was made or not, we do know that Conan Doyle agreed to have his name put forward and this information would have been conveyed to the committee and placed on the agenda for the AGM.

Apart from the motives mentioned above there were other possible reasons for the approach to Conan Doyle. Byrne's conduct the previous year had clearly caused a split in the society and the other committee members quite possibly feared an exodus of members (and with them the loss of a considerable amount of revenue) if nothing was done. It is therefore equally possible that some members of the society saw Conan Doyle as a unifying candidate who was too new to the society to be perceived as being part of either the pro or anti Byrne factions (and consequently equally acceptable to both sides). It is also tempting, if a touch cynical, to think that his fame as the creator of Sherlock Holmes came into play with some members seeing his occupancy of the top position as a way of securing greater publicity for the society as a whole.

Conan Doyle was in fact, despite his status as a relatively new member, a very good candidate for the position of president.

Unlike Reverend Rice Byrne he had significant literary and scientific credentials[46]. The former were obviously derived from his successes with the likes of *The White Company*, *Micah Clarke* and the Sherlock Holmes stories. The latter came from his experience as a medical doctor. He also had in his favour the fact that he had served on the committee of the Portsmouth Literary and Scientific Society in the capacity of joint-secretary and was therefore already familiar with how such a society was run.[47]

The official records of the society appear to be lost so we have to rely on the occasional reports given in *The Norwood News*[48]. Unfortunately it is clear that the management of the newspaper did not consider the society to be of particular interest and, as can be seen from articles throughout 1890 - 1891, the society only got a mention if it played host to a distinguished or controversial guest speaker (as with Annie Besant). Its internal elections and other affairs were simply not deemed newsworthy. This in itself lends some weight to the idea that Conan Doyle as president was seen as a way of changing this state of affairs.

In mid-May 1892 the annual general meeting took place. *The Norwood News* chose, as per usual, not to cover the event so we do not know the full agenda but we do know from subsequent

---

[46] Byrne was not entirely without literary experience. He had edited a collection of sermons and written a number of academic papers. His papers are available today through the University of Oxford.

[47] *A Study in Southsea* by Geoffrey Stavert (Chapter 5).

[48] The earliest UNLSS records held at Croydon Library date from 1909.

reports[49] that it was during this meeting that Conan Doyle was successfully appointed president of the society[50]. Williams was elected vice-president and Buchanan was re-elected as secretary[51].

It seems unlikely that Reverend Rice Byrne would have stood against Conan Doyle for the position. In his capacity as chairman he would probably have known that Conan Doyle was standing against him (and therefore that there was support for his candidature amongst the society membership and committee) and whilst he was probably still convinced of his moral superiority in the Annie Besant debate he could not overlook the letters of protest against him in *The Norwood News*. Despite his intolerance of other beliefs he was not so blinkered that he could not see that defeat was probable. In view of this it seems likely that, in an effort to save face, he officially stood down at the meeting (or earlier) and allowed Conan Doyle to be appointed unopposed. His name does not appear in any subsequent reports

---

[49] The issues of *The Norwood News* from May 1893 (see later).

[50] This rather significant event does not seem to have found its way into any letters to his mother or any other members of his family. As with his Norwood cricketing activities, Conan Doyle's involvement in the UNLSS was either deemed by him not to be worthy of mention or is contained within lost letters.

[51] Williams may have been vice-president or vice-chairman in 1891 (and therefore re-elected to that post in 1892) but records do not exist to prove this. It is clear that he was on the committee in 1891 or he would not have been part of the sub-committee that arranged the Annie Besant debate but there is no proof that he occupied a senior post at that time.

on the society's activities and it therefore seems likely that he left the society soon after the AGM. It must have been extremely galling to this aged clergyman to be replaced by a man who was nearly half his age[52].

It was almost certainly the events surrounding the UNLSS that caused Conan Doyle to temporarily neglect his cricketing commitments. The Norwood club's first fixture of the 1892 season was at home against Sutton but Conan Doyle did not play. In fact, according to *The Norwood News*, Conan Doyle did not turn out for his club until May 14th (almost certainly days after the UNLSS AGM) when he played at home against Croydon. This was a game of contrasting fortunes for him as although he bowled out five members of the Croydon side he himself was bowled out for nought.

On June 16th Conan Doyle's membership of the Reform Club in London was confirmed[53]. It was around this time that he was busy writing *Silver Blaze*, *The Cardboard Box* and *The Yellow Face* the latter two of which are set within a very small distance of South Norwood (Croydon and Norbury respectively). Five days before this on June 11th (and reported in *The Norwood*

---

[52] According to the Surrey History Centre, Byrne also ceased to be an inspector of schools in this year. Presumably at the age of sixty-four he had decided to retire.

[53] As previously mentioned, he had applied to join in October the previous year.

News of June 18th) a dead body was discovered almost on his doorstep.

According to the article, the body of a 'fully-developed female child' was found at approximately 8.30am in a field adjacent to Tennison Road quite near to the railway bridge (less than five minutes walk from Conan Doyle's house). The body was wrapped in fabric and tied up with tape and worsted (a type of yarn). This grisly parcel was opened by a woman who worked for Brock's firework factory who spotted it on her way to work. The article does not state the woman's reaction but we can to a certain extent infer that she was rather clinical about her discovery from what happened next.

The subsequent events, as described in the article, highlight how little attention was paid to crime scenes at this time in history. A man was waylaid by the discoverer of the body and dispatched in his cart for the police. PC 480W (names of constables were not always released in these articles) made his way to the scene and, according to the article, was physically handed the body by the woman who had found it. He is then reported as taking it back to South Norwood police station. There is nothing to suggest that any police presence was left at the scene and therefore nothing done to preserve any evidence that may have been there.

Dr. Carruthers of nearby Selhurst Road examined the body at the station and from the age and lack of violent marks concluded that the child had been born alive quite recently but had been allowed to starve. He further concluded that the child had been dead for four days. The same article was able to state that, based on the limited evidence available, the inquest had returned an open verdict pending further details from the police investigation. The article highlights a difference between reporting today and in Conan Doyle's time. We can be quite certain that if a dead body was discovered today in close proximity to the home of a famous author (and an author of detective stories at that) it would be mentioned regardless of its relevance[54].

It is interesting to speculate as to whether the real-life story of a body being parcelled up and left so close to his home could have had any influence on Conan Doyle's story of severed ears being packaged up and mailed to Miss Cushing. Even if there was no such link it was an interesting coincidence.

The same issue of *The Norwood News* carried a story referring to the closure of a fund that had been set up a short while earlier to raise money for the widow of the local station master. The fund had been started by local businessman and personality William Stanley. Stanley was, at least at a local level, a more famous figure than Conan Doyle[55] and would go on to contribute much to the lives of the people of South Norwood. Such acts of philanthropy as the fund were very much in his nature and he had, in September 1891, also paid for the erection of a new bandstand on South Norwood's recreation ground.

---

[54] The article also referred to the fact that this was not the only child's body to have been found in recent weeks. Another body had been found near Selhurst Road previously and had clearly suffered a violent death. It was not determined whether or not the two deaths were linked.

[55] Stanley is still revered in South Norwood today. A clock tower near to the station, paid for by local residents, was erected to commemorate Mr and Mrs Stanley's fiftieth wedding anniversary. The community halls are still known as the Stanley Halls and the adjacent school was, until quite recently, known as Stanley Technical College.

Part of South Norwood Recreation Ground in 2009. In many respects it answers to the description of the location where the parcelled up child's body was found. 12 Tennison Road is approximately five minutes walk away

William Stanley c1890 - More famous locally than Conan Doyle
(Courtesy of Croydon Local Studies Library)

The article stated that the fund had been wound up in order that the money raised could be passed on. It also listed the donors in order of amount donated. Stanley was at the head of the list with a donation of one pound and one shilling. Curiously there was no mention of a donation by Conan Doyle. It seems almost inconceivable that a man as famous as Conan Doyle would not have been approached. Given his ingrained sense of gallantry we can be reasonably certain that he would have contributed if he had been asked. We are therefore forced to assume that he was not asked. This in itself tells us something about the relationship between South Norwood and Conan Doyle. It suggests that while he was no doubt seen as a famous author and personality he was not seen as approachable by local residents and that perhaps he had not been embraced by the community as a whole[56].

Returning to William Stanley, it seems that despite the small size of South Norwood its two most famous residents had little or nothing to do with each other. This seems odd as they had much in common. Like Conan Doyle, Stanley was a prolific author and had a scientific background. Both men also shared an interest in photography with Stanley going so far as to author a book upon the subject - *Photography Made Easy* (1872).

The Upper Norwood Literary and Scientific Society would have been a natural organisation for Stanley to join but he appears not to have done so. The various articles concerning the society that appear in *The Norwood News* mention Conan Doyle but never mention Stanley. It seems unlikely that they would have failed to have mentioned him if he were a member so it is fairly safe to assume that he was not[57]. Perhaps Conan Doyle's

---

[56] This would explain the apparent lack of interest in Conan Doyle in South Norwood today. Perhaps his tendency to spend a lot of his time in Upper Norwood had a lot to do with the situation.

[57] Stanley's own autobiography and other books about his life held in Croydon Library also fail to make any mention of the society. They do however mention many other societies that Stanley was a member of. This further adds to the suggestion that he was not a member of the UNLSS.

frequent absences from South Norwood in connection with his writing and Stanley's many commitments ensured that the two men never met. However they would certainly have read about each other in the local press as both men received coverage on a semi-regular basis.

The issue of *The Strand* published in August 1892 carried the article *A Day with Dr. Conan Doyle* written by Harry How. How was a regular contributor to the magazine and had interviewed other personalities of the day such as W.S. Gilbert (of Gilbert and Sullivan fame). How's interview was by no means the first that Conan Doyle had given since arriving at Tennison Road. In May he had given an interview to *The Bookman* entitled *A Talk with Dr. Conan Doyle*[58]. However How's article ended up being the more memorable (and hence referenced) of the two.

After a brief tour of the house and garden, in the company of Conan Doyle and his wife, How and his host adjourned to the latter's study[59] and conducted the interview over a few cigars. That the interview was wide ranging was evident from the

---

[58] *Arthur Conan Doyle: A Life in Letters* edited by Jon Lellenberg et al.

[59] In his biography of Conan Doyle, John Dickson Carr states, ambiguously, that Conan Doyle's study in Tennison Road was to the left of the front door. Specifically it was to the left as viewed from the inside. If you examine the earlier photograph of the outside of the house (page 21) and compare the location of the chimney with that in the picture of the study (see below) this becomes clear.

resultant article. Conan Doyle's early life was briefly covered as were his experiences in the Arctic and Africa with How remarking that trophies of Conan Doyle's Arctic adventures were to be found in the dining room. When Conan Doyle went on to discuss his early medical career he demonstrated that his memory could be unreliable by referring to his ophthalmic practice being located in Wimpole Street whereas it was in fact in *Upper* Wimpole Street[60].

The principal aim of the article, from the perspective of How and *The Strand*, was to discuss Conan Doyle's writing and to focus on Sherlock Holmes in particular. This was not at all surprising as Newnes and Greenhough Smith clearly had an interest in the article being so focused. Only two months earlier *The Copper Beeches* had been published bringing the initial twelve adventures of Sherlock Holmes to an end. Holmes fever was at its height and *The Strand* needed to play to its audience and assure them that more was on the way. In order to achieve this Conan Doyle was asked by How about the future of Holmes and was assured that not only was there enough material for another Holmes series but also that the first story of that series[61] was 'of such an unsolvable character...' that Conan Doyle had bet his wife a shilling that she could not guess the solution. He also

---

[60] In his autobiography Conan Doyle changed the address again saying that his practice was at 2 Devonshire Place. This caused many problems years later when the Arthur Conan Doyle society sought to have a plaque erected to commemorate the site where the earliest Holmes short stories were written.

[61] *Silver Blaze.*

discussed the inception of Holmes and stated that his tutor Dr Joseph Bell was the inspiration.

This was quite a scoop for How. Conan Doyle had previously made plain in his *Bookman* interview that Sherlock Holmes was based on one of his university tutors but had not been more specific. How lost no time in capitalising on this new information. After the interview was concluded he wrote to Dr. Bell seeking further details. Bell responded and How was so pleased with the response that he published it along with his main article[62].

The article would certainly have been enough to placate *The Strand*'s Holmes fans and thus achieve the aim of Newnes and Greenhough Smith but they could not have it all their own way. Conan Doyle also discussed his other works and clearly spoke about *The White Company* at some length as the article devoted several paragraphs to its composition. In contrast the composition of *A Study in Scarlet* and *The Sign of Four* was covered in a few sentences. In some respects the balance of the article was much the same as the film of Conan Doyle, from a few years before his death, where he was forced to discuss Sherlock Holmes's inception in exchange for a platform to talk about his involvement in the Spiritualist movement.

---

[62] Bell was subsequently acknowledged by Conan Doyle as the inspiration for Holmes in the opening pages of *The Adventures of Sherlock Holmes* which contained Holmes's first twelve adventures and was published by George Newnes in October 1892.

The Elliot & Fry photo of Conan Doyle's study at 12 Tennison Road where the Harry How interview took place (Strand August 1892)

The Norwood News of August 27th 1892 carried an interesting reference to Conan Doyle in its *Notes of the Week* section.

Our neighbour, Mr Conan Doyle, has undertaken to write a story of 3,000 words for Phil May's Christmas Annual. Gossip - which in this case is likely to be accurate - has it that Mr Doyle is to get £50 for his story. Perhaps this is the largest sum the author of "Sherlock Holmes" has, during his brilliantly successful career, received for a single short story. Perhaps, too, it is a high-water mark in what can only be called the popular value of the English short story.

The article is quite interesting. Firstly, the writer had got the name of the publication wrong. It was actually called, according to Richard Lancelyn Green's bibliography of Conan Doyle, *Phil May's Illustrated Winter Annual*[63] and it was published in November. The same source also reveals that the short story in question was *Jelland's Voyage* [64].

---

[63] This was the first issue of this annual. It was to run for thirteen winter editions and three summer editions. (Source: Australian Dictionary of Biography - Online Edition).

[64] The story was subsequently re-published, with others, in a book entitled *Round the Fire Stories* in 1908. This volume also contained the 1898 stories (from the July and August issues of *The Strand* respectively) entitled *The Man with the Watches* and *The Lost Special* both of which are considered to be part of the Holmes apocrypha.

The suggested fee of fifty pounds merits some attention. The article refers to it as gossip but from where would such gossip have emanated? On October 14th 1891 Conan Doyle had written to his mother regarding *The Strand*'s request for an additional six Sherlock Holmes stories[65] (making up the twelve that constitute the first series - *The Adventures of Sherlock Holmes*). In his letter he states that he had determined to only write them if he was paid fifty pounds per story - irrespective of length. It is therefore tempting to suggest that he had adopted this as a standard fee for a short story rather than the sum being an offer made by the publishers of the annual. Perhaps he had mentioned this figure personally to the reporter as a way of publicly stating his price to other potential publishers. This would account for the article referring to the gossip's accuracy as being 'likely'.

September brought the end of Conan Doyle's first full season as a part of the Norwood Cricket Club. To round off the season he organised a team that was, according to *The Norwood News* of September 10th, 'composed of literary and artistic contributors to *The Idler* magazine.' Jerome K. Jerome attended but did not play. The article stated that 'the popular author of "Three Men in a Boat" was officiating as scorer for the Idlers.'[66]

---

[65] *Arthur Conan Doyle: A Life in Letters* edited by Jon Lellenberg et al.

[66] According to *The Norwood News* and *The Croydon Guardian*, this match took place on Wednesday September 7th. Georgina Doyle, in her book *Out of the Shadows*, states that it took place on Tuesday September 6th. Regrettably the newspaper cutting from which Mrs Doyle obtained this information is missing its header so its name is not known.

Despite atrocious weather the game was a good one. Conan Doyle, who played for the Idlers, only managed seventeen runs before being bowled out. When the Norwood team went into bat he was responsible for bowling out four of them. In the end the match was a close one with the Idlers scoring a total of 150 runs only thirteen more than their hosts[67].

The Norwood News, in its usual summing up of the season, reported that Conan Doyle had managed to accumulate the largest number of runs for his team that year having scored 524[68]. He was, the paper stated, 'the most consistent bat.' The assessment was certainly an improvement on that from 1891.

---

[67] *The Norwood News* report and other details on the match can be seen in appendix B.

[68] Conan Doyle took the names of many people in his stories from real people that he had met. In his sixth Sherlock Holmes short story, *The Man with the Twisted Lip*, we are introduced to Inspector Bradstreet. Interestingly, the name W.S. Bradstreet appears in the 1892 cricket summary. This could simply be a coincidence but if this Bradstreet was a member of the Norwood Cricket Club in 1891 it is perfectly possible that Conan Doyle could have met him soon after joining in June and later used his name in the Sherlock Holmes story, which he sent to his agent in August 1891. Coincidentally (or possibly not) a William S. Bradstreet (born in Surrey c1863) appears in the 1891 census as a resident in London.

Conan Doyle and Louise outside 12 Tennison Road. Conan Doyle's study windows are visible on the right. The curtains clearly match those of the earlier picture (The Strand August 1892)

Phil May (self portrait) date unknown but certainly late nineteenth century

Alfred Tennyson, 1st Baron Tennyson (1809 – 1892)

October 12th 1892 saw Conan Doyle's attendance at the funeral of Alfred Tennyson. The event, which was reported on in *The Times* of the following day, was also attended by many other famous literary names some of whom Conan Doyle was already on good terms with. Curiously most of these names were listed together and it is tempting to wonder whether or not this was pure coincidence. The relevant names in the article appeared in the following order:

Rev. S. Baring-Gould
Mr. Conan Doyle
Mr J.M. Barrie
Mr A. Russel Wallace
Professor Boyd Dawkins[69]
Mr James Payn

Leaving aside Baring-Gould and Barrie, who have been covered, we have James Payn who, as editor of *The Cornhill*, had serialised Conan Doyle's *The White Company* and Alfred Russel Wallace who was a famous British naturalist most noted for devising his own theory of natural selection independently of Charles Darwin. He is also interesting as he shared a good deal in common with Conan Doyle. They both had a scientific background, both were prolific authors[70] and both had a strong interest in Spiritualism. Wallace's writings went as far as to suggest that science and spiritualism were by no means mutually exclusive and this view would have been one that Conan Doyle

---

[69] Professor Dawkins does have a link (albeit tenuous) with Conan Doyle. Dawkins was involved in some of the investigations into Piltdown Man. This was the archaeological find that it was rumoured that Conan Doyle had a hand in faking. Details of Dawkins' involvement can be found in the book *The Antiquity of Man* by Arthur Keith which was first published in 1915.

[70] According to the Bibliography of the Published Writings of Alfred Russel Wallace (1823–1913) (hosted on the Internet by Western Kentucky University), Wallace wrote twenty-two books and in excess of seven hundred papers. A percentage of these papers concerned Spiritualism.

would have embraced. Sadly it was to be the fate of both men that their reputations suffered both during their lifetimes and after their deaths because of their faith in this emerging religion[71].

Alfred Russel Wallace (date unknown)

November brought the event that, for him at least, defined Conan Doyle's time in Norwood. The 15th saw the birth of his first son - Kingsley. The only child of Conan Doyle to be born in Norwood, he was christened at St. Marks Church, at the time the nearest church to Conan Doyle's house, on December 22nd. The full name given to his son was Arthur Alleyne Kingsley Conan

---

[71] Wallace had become an honorary member of the SPR in 1883. Tennyson became an honorary member the following year.

Doyle but he was known as Kingsley. On the paperwork Conan Doyle's occupation was listed, somewhat ambiguously as 'Gentleman'. Perhaps to his mind this sounded superior to 'Writer'.

In their December 31st issue *The Norwood News* carried, as usual, a range of commercial advertisements. Amongst these was one for a South Norwood stationers trading under the name Marris & Revene. Their advert clearly showed a bias towards their famous local author as a section (approximately one third of the entire advert) existed that was devoted solely to his works.

Dr. A. Conan Doyle's Works :—
Sherlock Holmes, 6/-; cash 4/6
White Company, 6/-; cash 4/6
Study in Scarlet, 3/6; cash 2/8
Sign of Four, 3/6; cash 2/8
Firm of Girdlestone, 3/6; cash 2/8
Micah Clarke, 3/6; cash 2/8
Captain of Polestar, 3/6; cash 2/8
The Great Shadow, 1/-; cash 9d.

LEATHER GOODS:

Blotters.   Desks.
Wallets.   Purses.

Excerpt from The Norwood News advert of December 31st 1892 for Marris & Revene Bookshop at 68 South Norwood High Street

South Norwood High Street c1900. The stationers Marris & Revene is on the left
(Courtesy of Croydon Local Studies Library)

St Marks Church 1905 - the site of Kingsley Conan Doyle's christening thirteen years before.
(Courtesy of Croydon Local Studies Library)

Conan Doyle and Kingsley in the garden of Tennison Road in 1894
(The collection of Brian Pugh)

1893

Re-election, demotion and literary freedom

For fans of Conan Doyle's most popular creation 1893 was to be a memorable year although they had no idea why as the year began. For them it was still a time of celebration with Sherlock Holmes having only just begun his second series of adventures.

The first story of the year, and the second in the new series, was *The Cardboard Box* which, as we have seen, was written by Conan Doyle about six months earlier and set in nearby Croydon. Its content was later to cause him some concern as it dealt with adultery and he was to insist that it was removed from *The Memoirs of Sherlock Holmes* when it was published by Newnes in December. The story was eventually placed into the series known as *His Last Bow*[72].

The first major event of the year from Conan Doyle's perspective was his decision to join the Society for Psychical Research which he did during January or very early February

---

[72] This has continued for most editions of the *Memoirs* since then. However, some publishers, such as Oxford World's Classics, have begun to return the story to its original place.

(see next illustration). Other books, which have stated that he joined in November, have implied that it was the death of his father that may have nudged him in this direction. However the fact that he joined at the beginning of the year, when his father was still alive, rules this out as the reason[73].

In fact it seems perfectly possible that existing member and UNLSS committee member A.C.R. Williams was, to some extent, behind Conan Doyle's decision to join. This seems even more plausible when you see that the same list of new members shows that the Secretary of the UNLSS, H.B.M. Buchanan, joined at the same time as Conan Doyle (albeit as an associate member)[74]. The UNLSS was now, either by accident or design, led by a card-carrying contingent of the Society for Psychical Research.

---

[73] If it was a death in the family that contributed to his decision to join the SPR it could have been that of his uncle James Doyle who died in December 1892.

[74] It is also clear, from SPR literature, that on occasion both Buchanan and Williams shared the same address - 9 Upper Beulah Hill, Upper Norwood. As Buchanan was at this address for many years the implication is that Williams lodged with him. The implication becomes a certaintly when you read a letter from Conan Doyle (reproduced in *Arthur Conan Doyle: A Life in Letters*) from January 1898 where he refers to Williams and Buchanan as having 'shared rooms'.

No. XCVII.—Vol. VII.　　　　　　　　　　　　　　　　FEBRUARY, 1892.

JOURNAL

OF THE

SOCIETY FOR PSYCHICAL RESEARCH.

NEW MEMBERS AND ASSOCIATES.

CORRESPONDING MEMBER.

PROFESSOR SABATIER, Montpellier, France.

HONORARY ASSOCIATE.

GOODRICH FREER, MISS A., Holy Trinity Vicarage, Glo'ster-gdns., W.

MEMBERS.

ASHBOURNE, THE LADY, 23, Fitzwilliam-street, Dublin.

DOYLE, A. CONAN, M.D., 12, Tennison-road, South Norwood, S.E.

SHARPE, JAMES W., M.A., Woodroffe, Portarlington-road, Bournemouth.

TANNER, SLINGSBY, 104B, Mount-street, Berkeley-square, W.

Part of the new members section of the February 1893 issue of the Journal of the Society for Psychical Research. It states that it is volume seven, but this is a misprint - it is actually volume six. Conan Doyle's name is second on the list of new members.

(Reproduced with the permission of the Society for Psychical Research)

ASSOCIATES.

ALLEN, MISS MARY GRAY, 14, Queen's-square, W.C.

BLACKBURN, ERNEST M., 31, Albert Hall Mansions, London, S.W.

BUCHANAN, H. B. M , B.A., 9, Upper Beulah Hill, Upper Norwood, S.E.

BUNNETT, A. SYLVESTER, 35, Whitehorse-road, Croydon.

COUSENS, CHARLES HUGHES, 7, Staple Inn, London, W.C.

COUSINS, A. F., Hotel Beaurivage, St. Moritz, Switzerland.

COWPER, THE HON. MRS. SPENCER, 38, Rue Jean Goujon, Paris.

DUFF, CHARLES E., M.B., 122, High-street, Deptford.

EUSTACE, JOHN N., M.D., Highfield, Drumcondra, Co. Dublin.

FURNIVALL, PERCY, Belgrave Hospital for Children, London, S.W

GARNER, EDWIN T., Glendale, Alexandra-road, Selhurst, Surrey.

HOLLAND, J. F. R., M.D., Kulm Hotel, St. Moritz, Switzerland.

JENKINSON, MRS. F. R. G., 112, Sloane-street, London, S.W.

LEGGE, THE LADY FRANCES, Woodsome, Huddersfield.

*The list of new associate members from the same SPR document. The third
name down is that of UNLSS Secretary H.B.M. Buchanan
(Reproduced with the permission of the Society for Psychical Research)*

Appropriately enough the UNLSS began the year with a lecture given by William Fletcher Barrett - one of the earliest members of the SPR. The lecture, given on January 4th and reported in *The Norwood News* of January 7th, was entitled *The Psychical Research Society.* Conan Doyle was in the chair for this meeting and personally moved a vote of thanks to Barrett[75]. On the 25th a lecture was given entitled *The Story of My Life.* It was presented by a Mr Felix Volkhovski, a Russian exile. Conan

---

[75] This same article referred to Conan Doyle as the president of the UNLSS. This was however not the first time that this had happened. An article in the October 22nd 1892 issue of *The Norwood News* discussed a lecture given on *War and its effects as seen in marine organisms.* It also described Conan Doyle as the society's president.

Doyle chaired and spoke at this meeting and voiced the opinion that the next war could destroy the Russian Government. One wonders whether Volkhovski's story and his own opinions on the perilous state of the Russian Government were the basis on which Conan Doyle's later Holmes story *The Adventure of The Golden Pince-Nez* was built[76].

The next event concerning Conan Doyle, reported by *The Norwood News,* concerned another meeting of the Upper Norwood Literary and Scientific Society. The article, published on February 25th, reported on a talk given by Dr. Bowlder Sharp on the 22nd entitled *Curiosities of Bird Life.* The article went on to state that Mr Williams[77] 'occupied the chair in the unavoidable absence of Dr Conan Doyle.'[78] This demonstrates that his occupancy of the post of president was definitely contributing to the increased press coverage for the society.

Saturday April 15th brought the Booksellers' Trade Dinner at the Holborn Restaurant. The restaurant appears to have been popular with the literary set generally and Conan Doyle personally. At the end of May 1892 Conan Doyle had been at the Holborn, along with such authors as H. Rider Haggard[79] for the annual dinner of the Society of Authors. The restaurant was also the location of the lunch between his characters Watson and

---

[76] This story featured a number of Russian exiles all of whom had involvement with a revolution in Russia.

[77] This was presumably A.C.R. Williams.

[78] The reason for his absence is not clear.

[79] Haggard was the author of *King Solomon's Mines*.

Stamford before they meet Sherlock Holmes in *A Study in Scarlet*. Now he was here again mainly, along with the other diners, to provide funds for the organising charity the Booksellers' Provident Institution. This charity, which had been founded in 1837, existed to provide for the needs of people involved in the book trade such as book sellers and even publishers. The charity also maintained a rest home in Abbots Langley in Hertfordshire for aged booksellers, booksellers' assistants and their widows.

The event was apparently important to Conan Doyle as he knew he was to speak and even wrote to his mother that it would be his debut speech in London. In the end it could not have been all that impressive a debut as *The Times* of April 17th summed up his entire contribution by reporting that after Sir H.E. Maxwell had made the toast to literature and a short speech - 'Mr. Conan Doyle replied.'

May 6th saw the start of the 1893 cricket season but, once again, Conan Doyle missed the opening game which was an away fixture against Carshalton. Ultimately he was not to pick up a bat for his club until the end of the month against Chislehurst and when he did so he only scored ten runs. It was not an auspicious start to his second full season but it is possible that his lack of attention to the match and the opening of the season in general had been caused by his less than happy involvement with the Savoy Theatre.

During 1892 J.M. Barrie had undertaken to write *Jane Annie* which was to be performed at the Savoy. The pressure the schedule placed on him induced a breakdown and he turned to Conan Doyle for help[80]. Always one to support his friends, Conan Doyle put his own work to one-side but found the task of finishing the play difficult as he was, to a certain extent, constrained by what Barrie had already written. Nevertheless he did his best.

Jane Annie opened on May 13th and both authors were in attendance in their own box. With hindsight both probably wished that they had had excuses not to show up. The audience gradually began to show its displeasure with the performance and this reached such a level that both Conan Doyle and Barrie felt it wise to slip away from the theatre to lick their wounds elsewhere.

Despite this unfortunate start the play managed to limp on for a total of fifty performances before closing and going on a brief tour. The failure was embarrassing for all concerned but especially for the Savoy's owner Richard D'Oyly Carte for whom it was his theatre's first failure.

Critics were predictably unkind. *The Times* of May 15th began on a positive note by stating that the plot was 'worthy of the traditions of the house' but went on to say that it 'lacks, however, the continual play of brilliant dialogue which is found in the best examples of the class, and many opportunities given by some of the most improbable situations seem to have been wasted.'

Equally predictably some of the strongest criticism came from Conan Doyle's sparring partner George Bernard Shaw who wrote in *The World* that it was 'the most unblushing outburst of

---

[80] *Teller of Tales* by Daniel Stashower (Chapter 10).

tomfoolery that two responsible citizens could conceivably indulge in publicly'[81] The news was not all bad however. *The Penny Illustrated and Illustrated Times* of May 20th was decidedly upbeat (to such an extent that you would be forgiven for thinking that its columnist had seen a different play). In the column *Music and Drama* the columnist, who went under the name of 'The Prompter', commented on the excellent performances of most of the cast, the standard of the sets and the quality of some of the songs. In particular a song entitled *A girl again I seem to be* was deemed so good that it 'should live for its own beauty'. The 'opera' itself was referred to as 'sparkling'. *The Graphic* of the same date was similarly pleased with the performance referring to the piece as 'well mounted' and the audience as 'brilliant'. Assuming these columnists stayed until the end of the piece it is decidedly odd that they did not report on the dissatisfied audience that other sources mentioned or the fact that the authors left the building rather than stay to the end.

---

[81] *Teller of Tales* by Daniel Stashower (Chapter 10).

Richard D'Oyly Carte (1844 - 1901) of the Savoy Theatre (from Vanity Fair)

*The inside of the Savoy Theatre c1890. On May13[th] 1893 Conan Doyle and
Barrie watched from one of the boxes as their play flopped before their eyes.
(Courtesy of The Gilbert & Sullivan Archive)*

Despite the poor opinion of his theatrical efforts in central London Conan Doyle's standing was in no way diminished back in Norwood. This was demonstrated on May 25th at the AGM of the Upper Norwood Literary and Scientific Society. *The Norwood News* of June 3rd chose to report on this event and this again reinforces the suggestion that the society's newsworthiness and profile had been enhanced by its famous president. Unsurprisingly, and presumably much to the relief of the committee, Conan Doyle was re-elected to serve a second term in charge[82].

Conan Doyle was not the only member to be re-elected. The vice-presidents (Keen and A.C.R. Williams), the secretary Buchanan and treasurer Dr Murray Thompson also continued in their roles. Three new members were also added in non-titled roles.

As soon as he was re-elected president Conan Doyle devoted time, as part of a sub-committee, to working out the syllabus of lectures to be delivered that year. He and his committee also instructed Dr. Thompson, who had reported the society's funds to be in credit to the tune of thirty-one pounds, to send a cheque to Dr Francis Campbell for £12 12s 'in furtherance of his work at the College for the Blind.'

---

[82] *The Norwood News* articles that report this and the 1893/4 lecture schedule can be seen in appendix B.

Anerley Hill (facing north-west) c1900. This was one of the two main access roads to Upper Norwood for people travelling from South Norwood (the other being South Norwood Hill). The view, with the Crystal Palace dominating the horizon, would be one that would have greeted Conan Doyle on those occasions that he used this route to attend UNLSS meetings. The Anerley Arms Hotel was about five minutes walk from this spot.

The college had been based in Upper Norwood for some years. Since October 1873 it had been situated in Westow Park which was just across from the Queens Hotel[83]. The donation was probably made for two reasons. Firstly the society had made use of the college's premises for delivering its lectures in the past and all of the lectures for the 1893/94 season were also to be delivered there. Secondly donating money to such an organisation probably gave some pleasure to the latent ophthalmic specialist in Conan Doyle.

June and July saw Conan Doyle very much occupied on the cricket front with no less than four matches each month. June saw matches against teams from Dulwich, Forest Hill, London & Westminster and Epsom. The first two matches brought victory for the Norwood team the latter two brought a draw and a loss respectively. July commenced with a draw against Croydon followed by three wins against Brixton Wanderers, Addiscombe and the Grecians. Curiously, for the latter two games Conan Doyle was listed as representing the second team. The apparent demotion is interesting and it appears that the reason for it was Conan Doyle's growing passion for golf. *The Norwood News* of September 23rd, in an article summarising the 1893 season, made plain that this was behind the demotion by stating that Conan Doyle after 'such great service to the club...' had 'fallen a victim to the allurement of golf and has, therefore, to a great extent, forsaken his old love.'

---

[83] *Heroes of the Darkness* by John Bernard Mannix.

A supermarket and community centre on Westow Street in Upper Norwood (2009). The College for the Blind occupied this area in Conan Doyle's time.

Exactly when Conan Doyle became interested in golf is something of a mystery. Most other biographies mention him playing the game in America and Egypt but few explore how and when the interest arose. Conan Doyle himself does not choose to enlighten us. His semi-autobiographical text, *The Stark Munro Letters,* appears not to mention the game at all and his autobiography, *Memories and Adventures,* waits until chapter twelve before referring to the laying out of a golf course in Davos, Switzerland. This was in 1895 when the interest was already firmly established.

So can we get close to pinpointing the date when golf entered Conan Doyle's life? It was on July 15th 1893 that Conan Doyle made his first appearance for the Norwood Cricket Club's second eleven. One month before this he was still playing for the first team so it would seem likely that the golf bug got the better of him somewhere between these two dates. Furthermore it is possible that Conan Doyle's first experience of swinging a golf club was in Norwood itself. Anecdotal evidence states that a nine-hole course was situated just to the north of South Norwood Lake and this would have been just visible from the cricket pitch[84]. If he did begin his golfing career on the Norwood course

---

[84] Rev. Eric Bailey, vicar of St John's Church in the 1930s and 40s, reported that his vicarage actually backed onto the course and that the vicar before him, Rev. H. Sutherland Gill, was an 'exceptionally good' golfer. The golf course was almost certainly in use prior to 1914 but it was then requisitioned for military use. It became available to golfers again after the war but then fell victim to the Second World War when petrol rationing meant that it was impossible to properly manage the

it is clear that, being only nine holes, it did not satisfy him for long and we know that he eventually joined the golf club at nearby Beckenham[85].

Conan Doyle never rated himself very highly as a golfer going so far as to say in *Memories and Adventures* that 'Personally I was an enthusiastic, but a very inefficient golfer...' John Dickson Carr tells us, in his biography, that Robert Barr, to whom, as we have seen, Conan Doyle was connected through *The Idler* magazine, referred to him as a 'golf inebriate' who practised golf in his own garden by trying to get balls into a tub that Barr considered to be 'rather too near the house.' This comes from the section of the book that deals with events from May 1893 to September 1893 and so largely corresponds with the cricket fixtures and the later *Norwood News* article.

Golf also enters the Sherlock Holmes stories around this time. Talk of golf clubs is briefly mentioned in the opening scenes of *The Greek Interpreter* which was published in September and therefore possibly written around July or August when Conan Doyle was playing his earliest rounds at Beckenham. It is clearly no coincidence that this is also where part of the same story is set.

---

grass and it began to grow out of control. (Source: The Norwood Society Official Website).

[85] *Conan Doyle: The Man who Created Sherlock Holmes* by Andrew Lycett.

Royal Normal College for the Blind - site of most UNLSS lectures.
From The Strand June 1891

For Conan Doyle a major literary task on his agenda was the end of Sherlock Holmes. He had originally wanted to bring about Holmes's demise at the end of the original twelve stories and only his mother's objections had dissuaded him. Now it was different - he recognised that if he ever wanted to focus his attention on other work he would have to bring about the end of Holmes.

Arguably he had begun this process months earlier when he had begun writing the story *The Yellow Face* in which Holmes's initial theory as to the solution was proven to be wide of the mark. Was Conan Doyle deliberately making Holmes less able in an effort to make the public like him less and make his end more palatable?

This possibility reared its head again in *The Resident Patient* where Holmes's initial decision not to act led to the murder of one man and the escape of his killers (although they are reported as very likely drowned at the end). The story which followed, *The Greek Interpreter*, continued along similar lines with one man dying and his killers escaping (as with the previous story the killers ultimately die but, again, this was nothing to do with the efforts of Holmes). Holmes was still largely successful but with no less than three stories in the series (or twenty-five percent) depicting him as partly failing it appeared as if Conan Doyle desired to damage the reputation of his own creation.

He commenced work on *The Final Problem* in March/April but it caused him problems[86]. He was to say on occasion that he always knew how his stories were going to end when he began them. He likened not doing so to setting out in a ship with no idea of where you were heading. The final Holmes story forced him to work slightly differently. He still knew that the story was to end with Holmes, as it were, leaving the stage but he was at a loss for the exact manner of his exit. All he realised was that it had to be dramatic[87]. It was the Reverend W.J. Dawson[88] who later recounted how, in August 1893 during a visit to Switzerland, he had suggested to Conan Doyle, with whom he had met up, that the Reichenbach falls was a suitable place for Holmes to vanish. The problem for Conan Doyle was that he had to take what he had written so far and steer it towards this new end. On his return to South Norwood he sat down to complete his story. He simply had to get his detective and anti-Holmes to the falls.

---

[86] On April 6th Conan Doyle wrote to his mother informing her that he was in the middle of the last Holmes story. Source: *Arthur Conan Doyle: A Life in Letters* edited by Jon Lellenberg et al.

[87] Dramatic effects were a mandatory requirement of Conan Doyle's work. In 1927 Greenhough Smith published a book entitled *What I Think - A Symposium on books and other things by famous writers of today*. In it, under the section *How I write my books*, Conan Doyle had written 'In short stories it has always seemed to me that so long as you produce your dramatic effect, accuracy of detail matters little.'

[88] *Arthur Conan Doyle: A Life in Letters* edited by Jon Lellenberg et al.

Despite his reputation, in the eyes of the public, as the first fictional master criminal, it is clear that Professor Moriarty was little more than a literary assassin. Conan Doyle had no long-term plans for him as a character. He simply existed to bring about the end of Holmes. Part of the success of Holmes had been down to the sheer believability of his characterisation. This was of course mostly due to the fact that he was based on Dr Joseph Bell. For Moriarty's character Conan Doyle took a similar tack. For him to appear a believable and worthy foe for Holmes he needed to come across as just a believable character and not as some moustache twirling melodramatic villain. The easiest way to achieve this was to also base him on a real person or persons.

The American Holmes scholar Vincent Starrett put forward the idea (which had, according to his article, come from Conan Doyle himself) that Moriarty was based on the international criminal Adam Worth (1844 - 1902)[89]. Worth started out as an Army deserter and eventually built up his own network of pickpockets. He graduated from this to organising much larger crimes culminating in the theft of Gainsborough's painting of the Duchess of Devonshire in 1876. A nod to the idea appears in the Holmes story *The Valley of Fear* where Moriarty is described as being in possession of a painting he could not possibly afford were he really only living on a professor's salary.

---

[89] This theory appeared in Starrett's regular column *Books Alive* in the *Chicago Tribune* of December 26th 1943.

Conan Doyle in 1893 - the year of Holmes's 'death' (from *Men and Women of the Day* 1893)

The parallels between Worth and Moriarty can be plainly seen but Worth was no academic or scientist. The source of this side of Moriarty's character had to come from elsewhere. The author Samuel Rosenberg, in his book *Naked is the Best Disguise*, suggests that Moriarty was based on the German Philosopher Friedrich Nietzsche. This idea was based, in part, on some similarities in their respective careers such as the fact that they were both elevated to University Professorships when quite young and that they were both subsequently forced to resign[90]. Needless to say there are plenty of other theories as to the inspiration behind this aspect of Moriarty's character.

Adam Worth. The inspiration for Professor Moriarty

The story written and dispatched, Conan Doyle simply got on with other work. He no doubt guessed that the story would be a shock to his fans. Little did he realise that the public would take the news far more badly than he had ever dreamed. However this was still in the future and for the time being it was not something he concerned himself with.

---

[90] See Rosenberg's book for full details.

Philosopher Friedrich Nietzsche - another possible inspiration for Professor Moriarty

A Death is Announced

On August 12th 1893 *The Norwood News* carried an amusing story entitled *The Adventures of Picklock Holes - The Bishop's Crime*. This, the first of a series of eight parodies, was written under the amusing pseudonym of 'Cunnin Toil'. The actual author's name was R.C. Lehmann and the stories were sourced from *Punch* magazine. The following week (August 19th) the second in the series, *The Duke's Feather*, was printed but after this no more were reproduced despite there being a further six to go. It seems unlikely that many British regional papers would have printed these stories so perhaps *The Norwood News* did so in the belief it would amuse their famous local resident. Little did anyone know that the subject of the parody was already out of the picture[91].

In the same month Conan Doyle's stories *The Great Shadow* and *Beyond the City* were published in book form by

---

[91] A second series of stories, predictably called *The Return of Picklock Holes* appeared in 1903 - the same year that Holmes officially returned from the dead in *The Empty House.*

Arrowsmith. One of the first papers to review both stories was the *Pall Mall Gazette* and, while it was enthusiastic about the former it had precious little time for the latter. In their opinion it was 'a story of quite uninteresting people...' and they concluded by remarking that Conan Doyle had failed 'to give it artistic justification.'

The September 30th issue of *The Norwood News* carried a lengthy article detailing the list of lectures that were to take place at the Upper Norwood Literary and Scientific Society. The author of the article considered it to be very appropriate for Conan Doyle, as president, to be giving the opening lecture of the season. This, held on October 4th, was *Some Facts about Fiction*. However the reporter who visited the lecture and subsequently wrote an article about it in the October 7th issue was clearly frustrated by Conan Doyle's insistence that the substance of the lecture be omitted from the article.

The article stated that 'It would have been a pleasure to publish a copious report of it...' but 'Dr. Doyle is, however, legitimately conservative of his rights as an author and lecturer...' In other words Conan Doyle expected payment from his lecture appearances and feared these would be adversely affected if the paper was allowed to report on the substance of his talk. The reporter instead had to be content with informing his readers that the lecture would soon be repeated in nearby Croydon and at other locations soon to be advertised. The article's final quote from Conan Doyle was that the novel, in his opinion, 'is the philanthropist of literature'.

A mere six days after the lecture, on October 10th, Conan Doyle's father Charles died aged sixty-one. He had been institutionalised (due to alcoholism and epilepsy) and thus absent so long from the day-to-day life of his family that it is hard to imagine the news being an unexpected or heavy blow to Conan Doyle. In many respects the news would probably have been regarded as a merciful release. While most other people would have turned their attentions to funeral arrangements Conan Doyle did not and chose to remain in Norwood. The reason for this was almost certainly the UNLSS lecture that was due the very next day.

This lecture was entitled *Recent Evidences As To Man's Survival Of Death* and was presented by Frederic Myers of the SPR[92]. Its content, which would definitely have been of interest to Conan Doyle under normal circumstances, was especially of interest in the wake of his father's death. Myers and Conan Doyle had corresponded on occasion since Conan Doyle's first letter on the subject of spiritualism in the magazine *Light* some years earlier and it is highly likely that the two men spoke about Charles Doyle's death (and 'survival') after the lecture was concluded.

October also brought bad news in the form of Louise Conan Doyle's health. She was diagnosed with consumption (or tuberculosis) and was given months to live. This naturally caused Conan Doyle to devote less time to his society duties as he channelled his energies into improving his wife's health. With the arrival of November came a number of lecturing commitments around the country. Many of us under similar circumstances would have been inclined to cancel such events but Conan Doyle, probably with Louise's support, decided to

---

[92] The exact content of this lecture is not known but it is likely to have been along the same lines as Myers' book entitled *Human Personality and Its Survival of Bodily Death*.

honour his commitments. He conveyed Louise to her mother's care in Reigate and then travelled around the country giving all of the lectures he had undertaken.

Also during November, an advert was printed in *The Illustrated Sporting and Dramatic News* which made use of Holmes and Watson as a means of selling Beecham's Pills. It is interesting to speculate as to whether Conan Doyle or *The Strand* received any kind of payment for this. Their permission certainly would have had to have been obtained in order for the names to be used. The advert was entitled *Sherlock Holmes and the Missing Box (With Apologies to Dr. A. Conan Doyle)* and was quite comical. It featured a short story in which Watson misplaces his pills and gets Holmes to solve the mystery. It ended with Holmes giving Watson some of his own pills and saying 'it is part of my system to use them in my system.'[93]

His lecturing over Conan Doyle collected his wife and they headed to Davos. Consequently he was not in the front line when the news of Holmes's end was broken to his adoring public.

---

[93] One of the many illustrators who drew for *The Illustrated Sporting and Dramatic News* was D.H. Friston. It was Friston who provided the first illustrations of Holmes, Watson, Lestrade and others in *Beeton's Christmas Annual* in 1887. Coincidentally the annual also contained an advert for the very same Beecham's Pills.

Frederic Myers (1843 - 1901). Poet, essayist and member of the Society for Psychical Research

Arthur Balfour (1848 - 1930) President of the Society for Psychical Research in 1893 and future Prime Minister of the United Kingdom (1902 - 1905)

December 1893 finally brought the day that was for Conan Doyle the official start of his freedom, for Newnes and Greenhough Smith a financial headache and for the reading public the biggest shock of their lives. *The Final Problem* was published[94] and the whole world learned of the death of their beloved detective. Throughout the world people read Watson's description of Holmes's apparent demise with a mixture of disbelief and anger. The publication of the story prompted Conan Doyle to write 'Killed Holmes' in his notebook under the December heading[95]. Even though he had finished the story some time earlier it seems clear that he did not consider himself to be truly free until he knew the story was in print. He almost certainly did not fully understand the level of public anger over his actions. To him Sherlock Holmes was, and always would be, the leading character from a series of second-rate stories that had got in the way of his literary ambitions.

We are told various stories about the aftermath of Holmes's disappearance. The tales about City men wearing black armbands and women wearing mourning dresses are well known but the mourning was not quite as universal as we are led to believe. *The Daily News* of December 13th was possibly the first

---

[94] Publication was possibly on the 12th or 13th as the earliest article the present author could find was dated the 13th (see later).

[95] This notebook became known as 'The Norwood Notebook' and was lot 20 in the Christies auction of Conan Doyle effects that took place on May 19th 2004. The notebook sold for £59,750 or $105,937. (Source: Christies' website).

to cover the momentous event. Their article began with 'Sherlock Holmes is no more. He dies with his name ringing in men's ears' and ended with 'Sherlock Holmes will not be forgotten by this generation at least.' Little did they or Conan Doyle realise how much of an enduring phenomenon Holmes was destined to become.

The newspaper *The Graphic* was also firmly on the side of the mourners with columnist H.D. Traill remarking, in its December 30th issue, that 'Everybody I meet is lamenting the tragedy of the last chapter in Mr. Conan Doyle's "Adventures of Sherlock Holmes" - I mean of course, the death of the hero.' He went on to speculate that Conan Doyle had perhaps brought about the end of Holmes in order to deny the actor Charles Brookfield any material to parody. Brookfield (1857 - 1913) was the first known actor to portray Sherlock Holmes on stage and had recently appeared in a Sherlock Holmes parody entitled *Under the Clock* which was playing at the Royal Court Theatre. Traill's penultimate remark was to say that 'a great cry of chagrin and disappointment has gone up from the world of light literature lovers at Sherlock's death.'

The Derby Mercury stood at the opposite end of the scale. Its regular column *Literature,* in its December 20th issue, stated that 'The public will hear with mixed feelings of the death of Mr. Sherlock Holmes, the celebrated detective, which occurs in this month's number of *The Strand Magazine*.' It went on to remark that 'He was a wonderful man, who knew a good deal about most things, except racing, but his wonderful cleverness got at last to be rather oppressive.'[96] The article's closing remarks noted that 'Dr. Doyle was, on the whole, perhaps wise in allowing him to be tumbled over a precipice' and that *The Strand* 'has other props than Sherlock Holmes.'

From the reaction of *The Norwood News* it could be considered that they shared the opinion of Conan Doyle and *The Derby Mercury*. Despite the fact that the death of Holmes was in newspapers worldwide, they elected to not even mention it in their December editions.

Much later, in 1898, at a dinner held in his honour Conan Doyle spoke about the final days of Sherlock Holmes stating 'when one has written twenty-six stories about one man, one feels that it is time to put it out of one's power to transgress any further.'[97]

This was complete nonsense and, deep down, Conan Doyle must have known it. He had after all done nothing of the sort. The plain and simple fact, which was clung onto by many Holmes fans after December 1893, was that there was no actual proof that Holmes was dead or, for that matter, that Moriarty was dead. There was no mention in *The Final Problem* of any bodies being recovered and the notion that Holmes was dead came from the conclusions drawn by Watson upon finding Holmes's note and alpine-stock by the falls. The very fact that it was Watson who determined that Holmes was dead gave people hope. After all, had Watson not been wrong many times before? It was

---

[96] This was a reference to the story *Silver Blaze* which contained a number of horse racing related inaccuracies.

[97] *Teller of Tales* by Daniel Stashower (Chapter 15)

Holmes himself who had said to Watson in *A Scandal in Bohemia* 'You see, but you do not observe.'

[Miss Lottie Venne and Mr. Charles Brookfield

Caricature of Charles Brookfield - the first man to portray Sherlock Holmes on stage
(Source unknown but possibly from Punch Magazine)

It is undoubtedly true that Conan Doyle was determined to write no more Holmes stories and had, as far as he was concerned, finished Holmes. However the manner of Holmes's 'death' allowed him the emergency option of bringing Holmes back at a later date without having to bend the laws of nature. He knew he could, as he ultimately did, say that Holmes had never gone over the falls and had simply been away for a period of time.

So why did he give himself this option if he was so tired of the character? The answer probably lies in his upbringing. His mother Mary had always drilled into him a chivalric sense of honour and sacrifice and Conan Doyle had taken this very much to heart. One of the ways this manifested itself was in the way he always put the security of his family first.

This attitude was summed up in a letter to his mother dated June 24th 1893 where he stated that 'I know of no pleasure to be had out of money save that of securing the happiness of one's family'[98]. The same letter went on to discuss the setting up of an annuity for his mother and insuring his life for one thousand pounds to ensure the security of his sister Lottie. His wife and children would be supported by his savings and royalties.

The temporary removal of Holmes from the scene gave Conan Doyle the breathing space he needed to focus on his other works but he knew as well as anyone that, despite his low opinion of them, the Holmes adventures had secured him the most reliable income and that he could conceivably need to dust down the character in the future should his non-Holmes works

---

[98] *Arthur Conan Doyle: A Life in Letters* edited by Jon Lellenberg et al.

not bring the financial security for him and his family that he considered to be so important.

This slight lack of confidence may have been triggered by an event that almost certainly occurred that same year. It seems likely, but not certain, that, in the latter half of 1893, Conan Doyle gave a reading to The Authors' Club. It was not a happy experience for him. He stood up to read a story called *The Curse of Eve*[99] which he had just completed. The reaction to the story was subdued to say the least. Walter Besant is reported to have turned to a *Daily Express* reporter - Ralph Blumenfeld - and enquired 'Have you ever heard worse?' The sense of disappointment felt by the club members can only have been made more acute by the fact that this story had come from Conan Doyle who, by this time, was one of the most famous and successful authors in the world.

He reacted to the criticism well. The poor reception had clearly shown him that more work was needed and he admitted to his mother in a letter dated May 2nd 1894 that he intended to change the story 'to make the woman recover.'[100] The story was published in the second half of 1894 as part of a collection entitled *Round the Red Lamp*. Unlike many of the other stories it was not published in any periodical before then down, presumably in part, to the fact that he re-worked it in the face of the earlier criticism.

---

[99] *Teller of Tales* by Daniel Stashower.

[100] *Arthur Conan Doyle: A Life in Letters* edited by Jon Lellenberg et al.

On December 28th *The Pall Mall Gazette*, which had not always been Conan Doyle's friend, decided to publish an interview with Joseph Bell. The reporter, whose name was not attached to the article, had been in Edinburgh to cover the Ardlamont trial[101] at which Dr. Bell was a witness for the prosecution[102]. No doubt seeing the opportunity to kill two birds with one stone he sought to interview Bell in order that he could have an article to tie in with the 'death' of Bell's fictional counterpart. According to his article the reporter initially had some difficulty getting Bell to cooperate. However Bell's courtesy eventually forced him to give way and he submitted to what ended up being quite a comprehensive interview.

The interview began with Bell confirming that he had assisted the police for over twenty years in similar cases to the current trial but that he was not free to discuss them. Unable to pursue this angle further the reporter instead turned to the subject of Conan Doyle. He asked Bell if he had seen any indication of Conan Doyle's literary abilities during the period that he had

---

[101] The Ardlamont trial, on the face of it, was an open and shut case. A young aristocrat named Cecil Hambrough had been found dead in woodland with a gun shot wound to the head. His tutor and another companion who had gone shooting with Hambrough were seen fleeing the woods after the gunshot. The tutor - Alfred John Monson, who claimed that Hambrough had accidentally shot himself, later attempted to gain access to money from insurance policies that he had persuaded Hambrough to take out shortly before his death. Despite the rather compelling circumstantial evidence a verdict of 'not proven' was returned which allowed Monson to walk free.

[102] The Scotsman on-line edition.

been his tutor. Bell replied that he had no idea that this would end up being Conan Doyle's line in life but did state that he regarded him as 'one of the best students I ever had.' He went on to remark that 'He was exceedingly interested always upon anything connected with diagnosis, and was never tired of trying to discover all those little details which one looks for.'

Despite knowing that the subject was off-limits, the reporter then attempted once more to get details of Bell's involvement with the police. He asked Bell what his 'exact connection with the Crown...' was. Bell appears to have taken this unwelcome persistence remarkably well and stated that he had no 'official' connection but that he simply assisted his colleague Dr. Littlejohn as and when required.

The reporter was not deterred and proceeded to ask 'Is there any system by which the habit of observation is to be cultivated - among the police for instance?' Bell, whose courtesy must have been pushed to its limits by his interrogator's determination, began his response with 'There is amongst doctors...' before voluntarily drifting back towards the subject of law enforcement. At this point he demonstrated an attitude towards the police that Holmes fans would have been bound to recognise. He stated that he was of the opinion that many policemen came up with theories and then shaped the facts to fit them. He went on to state that 'You cannot expect the ordinary bobby, splendid fellow as he is so far as pluck and honesty go, to stand eight hours on his legs and then develop great mental strength. He doesn't get enough blood to his brain to permit of it.'

Despite this low opinion of the intelligence of the rank-and-file police, Bell, like Holmes, did rate some of them. He had high praise for Inspector Greet, who had come up from London to work on the Ardlamont case. Bell considered Greet to be 'a very smart officer.'

1894

Severing the ties

On January 6th *Tit Bits* magazine produced an article on the death of Sherlock Holmes. The author stated, with regards to Conan Doyle 'that he will, at some future date, if opportunity may occur, give us the offer of some posthumous histories of the great detective.'[103]

A mere few months after finishing *The Final Problem* and only a matter of weeks after its publication Conan Doyle was already holding out the possibility of further, albeit pre-Reichenbach, adventures for his most popular character. As the next Holmes adventure, the famous *Hound of the Baskervilles*, was not to appear until 1901 what are we to make of this statement? One interpretation is that Conan Doyle had been so shocked by the reaction to Holmes's apparent demise that he held out the possibility of further adventures as a means of calming down his enraged readers (and perhaps preventing them from deserting him). With hindsight this suggestion of further

---

[103] *A Bibliography of A. Conan Doyle* by Richard Lancelyn Green and John Michael Gibson.

adventures was rather cruel on Conan Doyle's part as he probably had no intention of doing any in the near future and all he achieved was to raise the hopes of legions of Holmes fans (not to mention the management of *The Strand*).

With the end of March came the end of the Upper Norwood Literary and Scientific Society's lecture schedule. The primary task facing the committee was the preparations for the annual general meeting in May. Aside from the election for committee posts the most significant event at the AGM would be the presentation of the society accounts. The big question for the committee was whether their president would take part in these preparations. After all Conan Doyle was at this time still in Switzerland.

In the end Conan Doyle and Louise, along with his sister Lottie, returned to England and Tennison Road in April. Shortly afterwards Louise headed to her mother's home in Reigate to see the children and Conan Doyle headed to the Reform Club leaving Lottie in charge of the house.

It seems probable that Conan Doyle communicated with the committee by some means during this period and informed them that while he would attend the AGM he would not be standing for re-election as society president and almost certainly would not attend meetings in the future.

This would have been a serious blow for the committee as the society had prospered, particularly in terms of media coverage, under Conan Doyle's leadership. It is also highly likely that his presidency had helped to attract more high-profile speakers. Attempts would no doubt have been made to persuade him to change his mind but they would have fallen on stony ground. He was to state later that his resignation was a result of his intention of spending future winters abroad. Whether he was candid with the committee and told them that this decision was due to his wife's condition is unknown. However, given the stigma attached to consumption, it seems likely that he kept this to himself.

The big problem with the announcement of the resignation at this time (assuming that this was indeed when he announced it) was that it gave the committee very little time to find someone willing to replace him. If they failed to do so they would be forced to seek candidates at the AGM itself. Secretary Buchanan put this matter high on his personal list of priorities. He had seen the benefits of having a high-profile president and he was determined to ensure that the next president could attract a similar level of interest.

The committee soon discovered that they had a second piece of bad news. A thorough examination of the accounts had revealed that the surplus funds were considerably less than they had been the previous year. The lectures were still well attended and subscriptions were still being paid. Where had the money gone?

This was not the first time that the society had faced such a mysterious shortfall. During the 1891/1892 season (the season during which Conan Doyle had probably joined) there had been a similar drop in funds and it was eventually discovered that this was down to the systematic abuse of family tickets. These were clearly designed to admit parents and their children to the lectures and debates but it seems likely that this had not been made explicit and people were using them to admit more than two adults. Perhaps in some cases they were even being used to admit people who were not of the same family[104].

As a result they appear to have been abolished at the beginning of the 1892/1893 season (possibly one of Conan Doyle's first acts as president). This had the desired result and the society's funds improved to the extent where they were able, as we have already seen, to make charitable donations from the surplus in May 1893.

The current shortfall was eventually determined to be down to the rising cost of hiring the hall at the college. The rise had not been sufficiently offset by the lecture admission fees and subscriptions with the inevitable result that the surplus was eaten into. The question now was what could be done to prevent this happening in the coming season.

It seems clear that the committee's first idea was to approach Dr. Campbell at the college and ask him if he would be prepared to reduce his fee for the hire of the hall. If the committee entertained any belief that the previous year's charitable donation might lead to a favourable response they were soon disappointed. Dr. Campbell made it perfectly clear that he was not prepared to lower the hall fees. He did however undertake to keep them at the existing level. This would have been some comfort to the committee but did not remove their immediate problem.

The committee also realised that their present situation could have potentially been even worse. Two of the lectures of the season had been given by lecturers who had waived their fees. The society had therefore made more money on these lectures

---

[104] It is possible that these financial problems also played their part in the exit of Reverend Rice Byrne in 1892.

than they would have done otherwise. If these two lecturers had charged for their services the society could very well have been facing an overall deficit. In light of all this the committee agreed that the subscriptions would have to rise to meet the extra cost as they could not count on fees being waived in the future.

Meanwhile, in the press, the absence of Sherlock Holmes was still causing the occasional rumble of discontent. Naturally, other writers had attempted to fill the void. Arguably the most famous and enduring of these Holmes 'replacements' was Sexton Blake who appeared to readers in December 1893 just as Sherlock Holmes exited the stage. It is interesting to imagine what Conan Doyle may have thought, if anything, about these imitators. In the immediate aftermath of Holmes's exit it is easy to imagine him being quite pleased that other characters had stepped forward. It may have occurred to him that, were they successful, people would stop asking him about Holmes or more Holmes adventures and leave him in peace with his other projects. However it may have also occurred to him that too many similar detectives could potentially devalue his famous creation and dent the income he could gain should he ever want to bring Holmes back. History has shown us that he had no cause for alarm but whether he could see this at the time or whether he even cared is debatable.

The success of Sexton Blake, often described as 'the poor man's Sherlock Holmes' was by no means guaranteed to other similar characters as was demonstrated on April 6th 1894. *The Pall Mall Gazette* of that day carried a review entitled *Sherlock Holmes as a Bore*. It was not an article about Holmes but about another would-be replacement. This time it was a female detective called Loveday Brooke who had appeared in a book of stories entitled *The Experiences of Loveday Brooke*[105]. Despite stating that the book was 'as good if not better than many volumes of this sort' the review went on to say that the recipe of the stories was invariable - 'avoid the obvious criminal: connect your case if possible with some absolutely irrelevant advertisement read by chance in the morning paper: score off everyone else around, but remember last of all that it is possible even for an amateur detective to be a bore.'

---

[105] Loveday Brooke actually appeared before Sexton Blake and before Sherlock Holmes's date with Professor Moriarty. As with the Holmes stories the Loveday Brooke stories first appeared in a magazine (in this case *The Ludgate Monthly*) in February 1893 before appearing in book form the following year.

An illustration from the Loveday Brooke story - The Black Bag Left on a Doorstep - Note the similarity to the Sidney Paget illustrations from both The Boscombe Valley Mystery and Silver Blaze

It appears that Conan Doyle did a lot of travelling between South Norwood and central London in the first week of May. We know that he was at the Reform Club on April 30th as he wrote a letter from there to *The Daily Chronicle* to protest at the ban imposed by W.H. Smith on the novel *Esther Waters* by George Moore[106].

---

[106] This was by no means the first contact between the two men. In early 1891 Conan Doyle's Napoleonic story *A Straggler of '15* had been published. Later Conan Doyle converted it into a play. We know that this was ultimately sent to the actor Henry Irving (more later) but, according to the author Hesketh Pearson, Conan Doyle sent it first to

The novel was one of many in that age that depicted the life of, so called, 'fallen women' but it was deemed unacceptable and immoral by the bookseller W.H. Smith who banned it from all their stores[107].

This unilateral censorship infuriated Conan Doyle and in his letter he remarked that 'Exclusion from their stalls and their library means that the work is cut off at the meter as far as the country consumer is concerned'. He rounded off the letter by stating that 'To draw a vice is one thing, and to make it attractive is another.' The letter was published on May 1st and prompted other papers to offer their own opinions. One of the first of these was *The Pall Mall Gazette* which stated, in an issue released on the same day, that 'We have had ourselves to suffer (the expression is purely technical) from Messrs. Smith, as well as to call attention more than once to the arbitrary and impertinent censorship they exercise over new books.' They followed this with an endorsement of Conan Doyle's position and went so far as to suggest, with regards to W.H. Smith, 'that their monopoly makes them an institution that should be controlled in the public interest...'

On May 2nd a response appeared from a supporter of W.H. Smith which challenged Conan Doyle's position. Not being one to back away from what he saw as a just cause he immediately wrote a response. This letter was written at Tennison Road that

---

Moore in order to get his opinion. Moore replied 'I do not know if your play would act - that is to say if a few alterations would fit it for the stage, ... but I do know that it made me cry like a child.'

[107] *Writers, Readers and Reputations* by Philip J. Waller.

same day (and was published in *The Daily Chronicle* on the 3rd). In it he countered his opponent by stating quite simply that 'If a book errs in morality let the law of England be called in. But we object to an unauthorised judge, who condemns without trial, and punishes the author more heavily than any court could do.' So impressed was Moore with Conan Doyle's support he wrote a letter of thanks which was published in the same paper on the 3rd.

Later that same day (May 2nd) Conan Doyle must have also travelled to the Reform Club as he wrote to his mother from there to see if she was following what he called the 'Smith-Esther Waters-Conan Doyle controversy'. In his letter he claimed that his latest letter 'knocks the bottom out of their defence completely.' This at least proves that he was at home at the beginning of the day and was at the Reform Club at the end.

During this time Lottie was supervising the redecoration of Louise's room, a subject that she wrote to her mother about on May 3rd. In her letter she remarked that Conan Doyle was very busy - heading out to town first thing in the morning and, due to a large number of dinner engagements, frequently not returning until quite late. Conan Doyle's desire to avoid the sickroom atmosphere of Tennison Road no doubt had a lot to do with his decision to spend time away but he also had a full programme of events that week.

George Moore (1852 - 1933) author of Esther Waters

In the evening of the 3rd he dined with the staff of the *Pall Mall Magazine* but it seems likely that he returned to South Norwood in the evening as he was to take Lottie the next day to the early private showing of the exhibition at the Royal Academy of Art and to the Independent Theatre. It also follows that he would have escorted her back to Tennison Road at the end of the day (not to do so would have been rather un-gentlemanly).

He was certainly back in central London on Saturday May 5th in order to attend the annual banquet of the Royal Academy of Art. This event, hosted by the Academy's president Sir Frederic Leighton[108], was covered widely by the local and national press[109]. However Conan Doyle was very much on the sidelines and does not seem to have merited a mention in the coverage the event received. Whether or not he stayed in London long after this is open to debate but he certainly headed back to South Norwood within the week as he had a number of local appointments.

The first of these appointments was the annual general meeting of the Upper Norwood Literary and Scientific Society which took place on Friday May 11th. Due to the meeting being held on the Friday the details were too late to feature in the next day's paper. Consequently full details were ultimately reported in *The Norwood News* of May 19th. The paper easily devoted the largest number of column inches to the society that it had ever done to date. Two articles appeared and both largely dwelt on Conan Doyle's exit.

---

[108] Leighton was made a Baron in the New Years honours list of 1896. Unfortunately he died the day after the patent was drawn up so he was easily one of the shortest living Barons in British history.

[109] The similarity of many of the reports suggests that they were all based on the same source.

*Sir Frederic (later Lord) Leighton - President of the Royal Academy of Art
(1830 - 1896)*

The meeting was held at 'the Welcome, Westow Street' which was in fact short for the Welcome Lecture Hall. This was the usual location for the society's AGM and was nothing to do with the hall fees for the use of the College for the Blind. This hall was a multi-purpose hall, situated above the Welcome Coffee Public House and used because its smaller size lent itself to the lesser number of people that attended the AGM.

The first article mentioned how the society had 'for two seasons enjoyed the privilege in having for its president not only a popular author, but a first-class literary man in the person of Dr. Conan Doyle.' The rest of the article continued in much the same sycophantic vein and conjured up some rather colourful imagery such as likening Conan Doyle to the figurehead of a ship and remarking that 'Dr. Doyle has directed and controlled the fortunes of the good ship in which a favoured few have made many pleasant voyages.'

Although consistently in favour of Conan Doyle, the article's author was clearly not so enamoured of the society itself describing it as a testament to Conan Doyle's 'zeal for the intellectual life...' that he was prepared to devote so much of his time to 'a body so imperfectly organised...' In view of the state the accounts had been allowed to get into this somewhat harsh comment was not entirely unwarranted. The article's author then went on to describe *The Norwood News* itself as 'the journal which alone has given due prominence to the doings of the society...'

The Foresters' Hall, Westow Street, Upper Norwood (2009) In Conan Doyle's time this was called the Welcome Hall and the UNLSS AGMs were held here, each May, on the first floor. It was here that Conan Doyle was elected UNLSS president in 1892 and 1893 and resigned from that post in 1894.The coffee house was at number 27 (the ground floor premises on the right).

The statement was rather disingenuous since the paper, as stated earlier, had barely mentioned the society prior to Conan Doyle's presidency (unless it had a famous speaker) and had continued to all but ignore the society during Conan Doyle's first term. It was only in May 1893 upon Conan Doyle's re-election that the paper covered the occasion and printed the full program of lectures for the 1893/1894 season[110].

The second article was more akin to minutes of the meeting[111]. The treasurer, Dr. Murray Thompson, was, for unknown reasons, unable to attend the meeting so the task of reporting on the less than ideal financial state of the club fell to Mr. S. Bromhead. He informed those present of the reduced surplus and told all members of Dr. Campbell's hall charges which 'he did not see his way to reduce.' This less than auspicious opening was followed by Conan Doyle formally announcing his resignation as president. He expressed his regret that he was abandoning the chair 'for at least some years to come...' and further stated that his memories of being president would always be a 'pleasant recollection'. The remarks suggest that, at the time, Conan Doyle was not contemplating a permanent departure from the Norwood area.

---

[110] *The Norwood News* resumed its lack of coverage of the society from this point on. The issues of the paper in October 1894 contain virtually nothing on the programme of events for 1894/1895 in stark contrast to the coverage following Conan Doyle's re-election.

[111] Part of this article can be found in appendix B.

A Mr. Judd then spoke to formally propose, with regret, that the resignation be accepted. He also noted that Conan Doyle 'had done most valuable service in promoting the prosperity of the society.' This remark almost certainly referred to the society's higher profile under Conan Doyle's presidency rather than its financial state which was the responsibility of the treasurer and not presently in the best of conditions.

The motion to accept the resignation accepted, Conan Doyle spoke and added to the impression that leaving the area permanently was not on his mind. He said 'I thank you very much. It is very kind of you. Though I have to leave, I trust you will keep my name on the committee so that at least I may have some little connection with the society.' This was met, according to the article, with much loud applause.

Naturally the next issue on the agenda was the election of Conan Doyle's replacement. A perfectly natural and sensible move would have been to appoint someone already on the committee such as A.C.R. Williams who had deputised for Conan Doyle before[112]. However the society had not given up on

---

[112] It is possible that A.C.R Williams was originally from Australia. The 1901 UK census reveals an Alfred Charles Williams, whose occupation was listed as solicitor, living in Streatham, only a short distance from Upper Norwood. His age was listed as thirty-six and his place of birth as Melbourne. At the request of the author some research was conducted and Steve Duke of the Sydney Passengers uncovered the birth certificate of an Alfred Williams, born in 1865 in Melbourne to William Williams and Elizabeth Pearce. The date of birth clearly corresponds with the age in the UK census and lends weight to the theory that it is the same man. All this raises the interesting possibility that Williams, as Conan Doyle's friend, solicitor and fellow SPR

its desire to have someone high-profile in the president's chair. It was time for Buchanan to report.

The Secretary stood and proposed that local Norwood M.P. Mr C.E. Tritton be elected president. Evidently Tritton must have been sounded out by Buchanan in the few weeks between the close of the lecture season and the AGM. He had accepted the nomination and had promised Buchanan that he would be happy to hold the office and, according to the article, 'attend as many of the meetings as he could.' The motion was seconded and carried but it must have been concerning to those present that not only did the president-elect not attend the AGM but that he also made it clear that he would not be a regular attendee at future meetings. Furthermore it is not even clear whether Tritton was a member of the society prior to his election although one hopes that he was[113].

---

member, could have directly or indirectly influenced Conan Doyle's later spiritualist tour of Australia.

[113] Tritton's non-appearance at the AGM, although not ideal, was probably not unexpected. The Cambridge educated politician involved himself in a great many philanthropic and religious organisations which probably left him with little spare time. Amongst other roles he was President of the Norwood Cottage Hospital. The events at this hospital were evidently deemed highly newsworthy as a status report on its doings featured in many issues of *The Norwood News* - something the UNLSS probably envied to a certain extent. Tritton remained a M.P. until 1906 and was made a Baronet in 1905. It is interesting to speculate as to what some members may have thought about another very religious man taking up the post of president after the experiences with the Rev. John Rice Byrne as chairman in 1891.

Conan Doyle endorsed Tritton's appointment remarking that he 'would make a most excellent president.' This implies that he was, at the very least, familiar with Tritton's philanthropic work and may have even known him personally. He went on to suggest that in his opinion Buchanan should be left in post as secretary. This was also approved and, in his absence, Dr Thompson was re-elected to the post of treasurer, those present being of the opinion that it was down to his care and attention that there was any surplus at all.

The final issue of significance to be addressed was that of future finances. It was stated that as the hall hire charges were remaining as for the previous year, the subscription would have to rise in order to preserve the same number and standard of lectures for the 1894/1895 season. The exact size of the increase was not discussed. Presumably this was deemed a subject for the new committee to address after the conclusion of the AGM.

The now ex-president declared that he considered it to be a good idea to reintroduce family tickets for lectures. In view of past problems this suggestion probably caused a few raised eyebrows. He also recommended, as a way of avoiding the abuses of the past, that such tickets should consist of four detachable sections thus ensuring that a family ticket only admitted four people. This, presumably, not only ensured that a family ticket would only ever admit four people but also that only two would be adults. The proposal was seconded and carried.

Finally a vote of thanks was offered to Conan Doyle and, in his response, he stated that in the recent fifty lectures he had given throughout England and Scotland he had found that it was common practice not to have a chairman present and therefore he as lecturer was rarely introduced properly or thanked at the conclusion. This was clearly intended as a compliment to the workings of the UNLSS. The secretary acknowledged the compliment and the importance of a chairman and the meeting was brought to a conclusion.

Despite his exit from the day-to-day affairs of the UNLSS Conan Doyle was in no rush to give up his cricket commitments. Perhaps this was, in part, motivated by his demotion from the Norwood first eleven the previous year. It is quite possible that he wished to regain his first team place before leaving Norwood.

If he did have a plan to regain his place it certainly did not get off to a good start. The season began on May 5th with an away fixture against Carshalton but Conan Doyle missed this due to the Royal Academy dinner. This ensured that he maintained his dubious record of never playing in the opening game of any full season at Norwood.

The next game that he could have played took place the day after the UNLSS meeting and was at home against Addiscombe however he did not play in this either. The first game he turned out for was on the following Monday (May 14th) when he played for Norwood at home against the London and Westminster Bank. Unfortunately his mind clearly was not on the game as he was bowled out without any runs.

Charles Ernest Tritton. MP for the Norwood Division of Lambeth and successor to Conan Doyle as president of the UNLSS (Spy 1897)

On May 25th *The Times* produced an article on a banquet that had been given the previous evening. The purpose of the occasion was to honour the crew of the United States Navy ship *Chicago*. Amongst the many military names was that of Conan Doyle. Quite why he had been invited to attend is something of a mystery. Was it due to the popularity of his Holmes stories in the U.S. or was it perhaps due to his known pro-American stance which had been unambiguously displayed in the Sherlock Holmes adventure *The Noble Bachelor* which had been published just over two years earlier?

In any event Conan Doyle was to witness Lord Roberts deliver a rousing speech extolling the virtues of the U.S. Navy, the *Chicago*'s captain and the areas of common interest between the two countries. This would not be his only brush with Roberts. He would actually meet with Roberts six years later, during the Boer War, to discuss the state of military field hospitals[114] and would be present at a dinner in Roberts' honour in June 1904.

On May 31st Conan Doyle took his sister Lottie to the Holborn Restaurant for the annual dinner of the Society of Authors. Many of the usual attendees were present including Walter Besant and the event was chaired by an editor named Leslie Stephen. *The Times*, in their report the following day, remarked that after Stephen had completed his introduction the society chairman Sir Frederick Pollock rose to deliver his own speech to the assembled members. This concerned the progress that was being made in securing appropriate copyright protection for British authors in Canada. After remarking that he was

---

[114] *Teller of Tales* by Daniel Stashower (Chapter 16).

hopeful that events were moving in the right direction, he proposed a toast to Literature, the Bishop of Oxford and to Conan Doyle. In Conan Doyle's case Pollock made special reference to the 'eminent position in literature' that he (Conan Doyle) occupied. It cannot have failed to please Conan Doyle to be publicly referred to in such glowing terms.

Sir Frederick Pollock (1845 - 1937). Chairman of The Society of Authors in 1894

On July 14th Conan Doyle appeared for the Norwood Cricket Club's first team in a match against Addiscombe but his next match, against the Granville team a week later, saw him once again making up the second eleven. The match after this, against Forest Hill, saw him resume his place in the first team. This alternation between teams is hard to fathom. However, it is possible that the club were trying to avoid overusing him in the run up to, what would end up being, his last international appearance.

This, which took place on August 6th, was a one day match against the Gentlemen of Holland[115] and was played at the Norwood ground. The visiting team won the toss, went into bat first and were all out for 134 with two of their players being caught by Conan Doyle. When the home team went into bat the result, according to *The Norwood News* report, was soon 'placed beyond doubt...' Conan Doyle came in for particular praise and, with a score of sixty-four, gained the highest number of runs of the entire match[116].

The newspaper's enthusiasm was not, on the surface, echoed by his club. The first match after this fixture, which was against the Spencer team, saw Conan Doyle once again appearing for the Norwood Second eleven.

---

[115] This was the term employed by *The Norwood News*. The team was referred to as the Gentlemen of the Netherlands in some other sources.

[116] It is well known that Conan Doyle commenced married life to second wife Jean Leckie in Crowborough in 1907. The location was chosen largely because Jean's parents had a home in the same area. However it is also interesting to note that, according to the Cricket Archive, one of Conan Doyle's Norwood cricket team mates, Leonidas de Montezuma, had been born in Crowborough in 1869 so he could have learned something about the area long before he moved there.

September 8th saw the last cricket fixture of the season for the Norwood side and the last time that Conan Doyle would play in the area. The match took place at the home ground and was against a side called F. Loud's XI due to the cancellation of the original match against Kenley. Loud was normally a member of the Norwood side but had formed a team of his favourite eleven from various clubs in order that a match could go ahead. It is not entirely surprising that Loud was the man chosen to form the opposing team. Despite being an excellent wicket keeper (he would take five wickets in this match) Loud was the poorest performing player of the season coming bottom of the table of batting averages and not even appearing on the table for bowling.

Unfortunately for Conan Doyle, on a personal level, his final match was no grand finale. He only scored five runs before being bowled out by G. Layman. The match however was a resounding win for the Norwood side.

The result was reported on in the September 15th issue of *The Norwood News*. In its summing up of the Norwood team's season the paper remarked that 'due to bad weather and other unavoidable causes, the local club have not had such a successful season as in former years.' Conan Doyle was mentioned as one of only three players to have scored a century and was also praised for his performance as a bowler.

However it is one of the article's other statements that is of particular interest. Conan Doyle's contribution to the season was summed up with the remark that 'The steady play of Dr. Conan Doyle has also been of incalculable service to the club on several occasions, and we much regret his intention of leaving the neighbourhood, as it will cause a serious loss to the cricket club.'

Only four months earlier at his last meeting of the Upper Norwood Literary and Scientific Society Conan Doyle had suggested that he might one day return to the role of president and had requested to remain on the committee in order to retain a link to the proceedings of the society. It would seem from the newspaper reports that no such similar undertaking was made with regards to the Norwood Cricket Club. It suggests that by this time he knew that he was unlikely to ever return to Norwood and therefore to give a similar undertaking would have been impractical. We can only speculate as to whether his earlier requests to the UNLSS were retracted.

The 21st September saw the premier of Conan Doyle's play *A Story of Waterloo*, starring Henry Irving, in Bristol at the Prince's Theatre. Irving had been in possession of the play since 1892 but had only recently found the space to put it into production. This was largely because the play, being one act, was too short to be shown without some other play to go with it. Irving finally found such another play entitled *The Bells* and was able to proceed.

The Times of the 22nd devoted several column inches to its review of the piece. Even though Conan Doyle's play was only the curtain raiser the article was entirely focused upon reviewing it rather than the piece it preceded.

The review was overwhelmingly positive with only a small number of minor criticisms. 'It is a powerful sketch...' the paper reported 'but, from its very nature, does not lend itself to that action which is the breath of life on the stage.' Another remark stated that 'the story turns on a pivot, instead of making progress.' The article continued with praise for the leading actors and concluded with 'The piece was received with enthusiasm, and Mr. Irving, in response to a call for the author, announced that Dr. Conan Doyle was not at present in England.'

Henry Irving (1838 - 1905)

By this Irving was referring to Conan Doyle's departure for the United States on a series of lecturing engagements. However Irving was slightly incorrect, although he probably did not know it. At the time he performed his play Conan Doyle was still in England. He was not to embark for America until the 23rd[117].

Conan Doyle's departure effectively marked the end of his association with Norwood. Knowing that he was unlikely to return to the area it is quite likely that he instructed his trusty solicitor A.C.R. Williams to oversee the onward sale of his Tennison Road lease. He was thus free of this responsibility when he returned from America and this allowed him to focus on making his home elsewhere.

---

[117] *Conan Doyle: The Man who Created Sherlock Holmes* by Andrew Lycett.

Beyond 1894

What Happened Next?

Arthur Conan Doyle returned from his travels and eventually moved to his new house 'Undershaw' near Haslemere. He was also persuaded, through a combination of public demand and financial rewards, to resurrect Sherlock Holmes. This was initially done in a pre-Reichenbach adventure called *The Hound of the Baskervilles* which was to become not only his most famous Sherlock Holmes story but arguably his most famous work of all.

In 1906 his wife Louise finally succumbed to her tuberculosis. The following year he married Jean Leckie whom he had met and fallen for only a handful of years after leaving Norwood. They elected to commence their married life elsewhere and settled in Crowborough in Sussex where Conan Doyle would eventually die in 1930.

According to local street directories 12 Tennison Road was unoccupied during 1895. According to the rate books for 1896 the house continued to be leased out to private tenants. The first of these was a William Mathley who occupied the house from 1896 until 1898. From 1899 to 1901 the house was again unoccupied before being occupied by a Reverend Henry Walker until 1905. At the time of Conan Doyle's death in 1930 the house was occupied by Arthur M. Hough.

James Payn continued as editor of *The Cornhill* magazine. Arguably Conan Doyle's most significant early supporter, he died in 1898 not long after Conan Doyle settled in Undershaw.

Herbert Greenhough Smith continued to edit *The Strand* magazine and be a strong supporter of Conan Doyle even when the latter started to be mocked for his spiritualist beliefs and belief in fairies. Greenhough Smith stepped down as editor of *The Strand* in 1930, the same year as Conan Doyle's death. He died five years later.

George Newnes lost his seat as MP for Newmarket in 1895 a seat he had held since 1885. In the same year he was created a Baronet and later re-entered parliament in 1900 as MP for Swansea. He retired from politics just before the 1910 election and retired to his home in north Devon. He died later that year aged fifty-nine.

Jerome K Jerome brought out a sequel to his hit book *Three Men in a Boat* but it did not live up to its predecessor. He volunteered to serve in the First World War but was rejected on age grounds but saw limited action as a volunteer ambulance driver with the French Army. He died in 1926.

Robert Barr retired as co-editor of *The Idler* magazine in 1895 but continued to write prolifically. He died in 1912.

George Bernard Shaw continued to be Conan Doyle's occasional opponent. In 1912 he published one of his most famous plays

Pygmalion which was later adapted into the musical *My Fair Lady*. He and Conan Doyle found themselves on the same side when they both opposed, unsuccessfully, the execution of Sir Roger Casement. He died in 1950.

Walter Besant was knighted in the birthday honours list of 1895[118]. This event was celebrated with a public dinner in his honour hosted by the Society of Authors. Towards the end of his life he worked as treasurer for the Atlantic Union an organisation dedicated to improving relations between Britain and the United States[119]. He died in 1901.

The Reverend John Rice Byrne died in 1907 - fifteen years after Conan Doyle had replaced him as head of the Upper Norwood Literary and Scientific Society. It would seem that he spent at least some of his retirement writing. His book *Lives of light & leading, biographical sketches of divines of the last three centuries* was published in 1904.

---

[118] This and other honours were reported in *The Graphic* on June 1st 1895.

[119] His involvement was mentioned in the *New York Times* of June 5th 1900. His pro-American stance very much tallied with that of Conan Doyle who never let an opportunity slip to talk up the common interests of both countries.

Post-Doyle Norwood

Due Recognition

The first recognition of Conan Doyle in South Norwood occurred towards the end of the Second World War. Farley Road, which connected Portland Road with Clifford Road, was causing some problems for the Royal Mail who kept confusing it with another Farley Road in nearby Thornton Heath. In order to prevent the situation continuing the decision was taken to rename the road in South Norwood as the man after whom the road was named - Thomas Farley - had stronger connections to Thornton Heath[120].

Many of the other roads that ran parallel to Farley Road were named after prominent local people. The most interesting of these being Balfour Road which was not, as one might be tempted to think, named after the former Prime Minister and Conan Doyle's fellow Society for Psychical Research member but was instead named after a corrupt local councillor.

---

[120] In addition to the road in Thornton Heath there is also a public house called The Thomas Farley.

After some time the new road name was unveiled. It was to be known as Doyle Road. The problem for the historian is that it is not definitively known whether or not it was actually named after South Norwood's famous one-time resident[121]. The probability nonetheless is high.

Doyle Road in South Norwood (2008)

Assuming, for the sake of argument, that it was, there was to be no further recognition for Conan Doyle from then until 1973 when the forerunner of English Heritage unveiled a plaque on 12

---

[121] Anecdotal evidence is strongly in favour of this explanation.

Tennison Road thereby formally acknowledging his residence in the area[122]. It is quite likely that the attempts from as early as 1950 to get a similar plaque erected at Conan Doyle's former ophthalmic practice at 2 Upper Wimpole Street in central London had raised his profile and ultimately led to this happening[123].

In January 1974 a school for children with severe learning disabilities opened in South Norwood on Tennison Road at the point where it connects to Selhurst Road and within one minute of Conan Doyle's former house. It is not known whether this actually had any connection to Conan Doyle's residency but the name of the school indicates either a definite link or a wonderful coincidence - it is called *The Priory School*[124].

On or about the same time as the school was opened an event took place which simply cannot be a coincidence. At 120 Selhurst Road a block of flats was erected. The building, which is between Selhurst railway station and Tennison Road, is called *Baskerville Court*.

Things then went quiet until July 1997 when a large mosaic, which had been constructed in the nearby Stanley Community

---

[122] This was one of the few occasions where Conan Doyle would be recognised before South Norwood hero William Stanley. Stanley's English Heritage plaque would not be unveiled for another twenty years.

[123] A Westminster council plaque was finally unveiled at 2 Upper Wimpole Street in 1994.

[124] As Sherlockians will know this is the fifth story in the series known as *The Return of Sherlock Holmes*.

Halls, was erected under the Portland Road railway bridge. It displayed representations of many aspects of South Norwood life covering everything from recycling to the local transport system. In the section devoted to the arts and education three names appeared - W.F. Stanley, Samuel Coleridge-Taylor (composer) and Conan Doyle.

Having read this one might be tempted to think that Conan Doyle is quite well commemorated in the area but it was (and to a certain extent still is) perfectly possible to pass through South Norwood and remain in ignorance of Conan Doyle's connection to the area. This was something the present author felt bound to address. The easiest way of achieving some progress soon presented itself.

It is a common feature of Public Houses up and down the United Kingdom that they feature old photographs of the area in which they are situated. Generally speaking, the era most commonly selected is the late nineteenth and early twentieth centuries. The watering holes of South Norwood are no exception to this rule with at least two pubs in the area showing a number of such photographs.

One of these is, predictably, named the William Stanley and it seemed only fitting that the pub named after the man whose reputation dominates South Norwood should also celebrate Conan Doyle and his works.

The Priory School at the end of Tennison Road (2009)

Baskerville Court on Selhurst Road quite close to Selhurst railway station
(2009)

A section of the mosaic in South Norwood with the names of Stanley and Conan Doyle shown (2009)

It was during the drafting of the section of *Close to Holmes* that deals with South Norwood that emails were being sent left right and centre to people at J.D. Wetherspoon whose pub the William Stanley is. Surprisingly they were very responsive to the idea and very swiftly came back with some suggested text for a display.

The hard work and nearly constant communication culminated in the display being erected on Tuesday May 12th 2009. Despite a few unfortunate inaccuracies the display is good and provides people with a good idea of Conan Doyle's connection to the area.

Some of the pictures that make up the Conan Doyle display in the William Stanley Public House, South Norwood (2009)

Appendix A - Norwood Cricket Season Summaries 1891 - 1894

In this section are transcriptions of the summing up of each Norwood Cricket Club season as presented in *The Norwood News*. They are shown as they were written.

Season, 1891

Notwithstanding the wet summer, and the consequent prevalence of difficult wickets, our local cricket club has had a most successful season, which is in a great measure owing to the infusion of some good new blood; not but what the "old stagers" have always been to the fore both with the willow and the leather when wanted. L. de Montezuma heads the batting averages, and well deserves the position, as he has batted most consistently throughout the season. In bowling also he has obtained the largest number of wickets, and has a good average.

There has been one score of a century made for the club - viz, 138 by S. Ellis, against Dulwich, during the "week"[125] Scores of 50 and upwards have been made as follows:

R.S. Rogers, 94 and 62; L. de Montezuma, 78, 62, and 52; W. Austin, 94; H.W.C. Bedford, 51; T.S. Gibson, 75; A. Springett, 52; F.S. Hallam, 77*; W.C. Elborough, 51, 75, and 51; S. Ellis, 50*.

Another new member, A. Conan Doyle, has also greatly assisted both with bat and ball. In the bowling, besides Montezuma, R.S. Rogers, W. Austin, and T.S. Gibson have done yeomen's service. The club is also to be congratulated on possessing two such good wicket-keepers as L.F. Elliott and C.A.V. Checkland, both of

---

[125] This refers to the Norwood Cricket Week. This occurred once every year and featured a game every day.

whom have been of much assistance to the bowlers behind the sticks. W.C. Elborough, unfortunately, was unable to help the club so much as usual this season, owing to ill-health.

Matches played, 43; won, 21; lost, 10; drawn, 12.

Runs scored by the club, 5,862, for the loss of 394 wickets, making an average of 14 runs per wicket.

Runs scored against the club, 3,899, for 375 wickets. Average, 10 runs per wicket.

* Signifies not out.

Season, 1892

Matches played, 44. Won, 20. Lost, 8. Drawn, 16. Runs scored by club 5,807 for 377 wickets. Approximate average, 15 runs per wicket. Runs scored by opponents 5,330 for 406 wickets. Approximate average, 13 runs per wicket.

As will be seen by the above figures, the season just over has been a very successful one for the local cricket club. The batting all round has been much higher than in any former year, seven members having obtained an average of over 20 runs per innings. There have been four individual centuries made during the season, viz: 115 by A.P. Roe, v. Forest Hill, on June 6th; 100* by L. de Montezuma, v. Addiscombe, on June 29th; 104 by C.A.V. Checkland, v. South Croydon, on August 1st; and 104* by A. Conan Doyle, v. Dulwich, on August 6th; and the following scores of 50 and upwards - W. Austin, 80*; C.A.V. Checkland, 71; A. Conan Doyle, 79; F.S. Hallam, 91 and 67; T.D. Lee, 97; and L. de Montezuma, 74 and 62*.

A.P. Roe heads the batting averages, but, unfortunately for the club, has only been able to play in 10 innings. Montezuma, this season, takes second place. He batted brilliantly at the commencement of the year, but fell off towards the close, partly from ill-health, but also from being somewhat stale, having played so continuously. The most consistent bat in the team has been Dr. Conan Doyle, who has obtained the largest aggregate of runs, and has played in the most innings, coming out with an average of just under 24 runs per innings. He has also obtained 44 wickets at a cost of a fraction over 10 runs per wicket. An old

Norwood cricketer, Harry Goodwyn, who is at home on leave from Ceylon, has been of great service to the club this season, both with the willow and in the field. It is much to be regretted (from a cricketing point of view) that Alfred Goodwin has shown such good form in lawn tennis, as it has taken him away from cricket, and deprived the club of his valuable services except in a very few matches.

C.A.V. Checkland, J.R Goold, and E. McCausland have all shown great improvement in batting this season. Of the new members, J.M. Capel and T.D. Lee have been great acquisitions, the former, by his brilliant batting and fielding, having materially assisted in many of the club victories, and the latter being chiefly remembered for his splendid innings of 97 against Epsom on August 13th, when the partnership of Dr. Conan Doyle and himself alone saved the club from a bad beating. It is unnecessary to mention the individual doings of such "old stagers" as W. Austin, F.S. Hallam, W.C. Elborough, and L.F. Elliott, as their averages will prove that no Norwood team could be considered complete without them. In the bowling department, R.S. Rogers comes out virtually top with the fine average of little over seven runs per wicket for 47 wickets. L. de Montezuma, A. Conan Doyle, Leslie Rogers, E. McCausland, and W.C. Elborough have all done good service with the leather.

Two notable bowling performances have to be chronicled, viz,: L. de Montezuma's six wickets for six runs in the first innings of Willesden, on the 6th July; and Leslie Rogers six Marylebone wickets for 10 runs on the 7th July. There has been much grumbling about the state of the club ground this season, the wickets having been very bumpy, but as there will be no football played there this winter, and the cricket pitch is to be seen to by some competent man, it is hoped that there will be no cause of complaint next season, and that the knowledge of this will lead to a further increase in the number of good playing members.

* Signifies not out.

Season, 1893

As announced at the end of last season, the cricket pitch at the Pavilion Grounds was successfully re-laid last winter, and perfect wickets have this season been the rule and not the exception, as in former years. This hot and dry summer has been a very trying one for cricket grounds, and much credit is due to the new ground man, Last, for the care and attention he has bestowed upon the club ground. In consequence, the rate of scoring has been very high, and the club has reached the highest aggregate ever obtained since its start in 1872 - viz., 6,088 runs for 353 wickets, or close upon 18 runs per wicket; whilst their opponents have scored 5,140 for 386 wickets, or just over 13 runs per wicket. The club has played 42 matches, winning 19, losing 8, and drawing 15; of which the first eleven have won 14, lost 3, drawn 12; and the second eleven won 5, lost 5, and drawn 3. Only one century has been obtained this season - viz., by W. Austin (100*) v. Brixton Wanderers on the 4th July.

The following scores of 50 and upwards have been recorded:- L. de Montezuma, 50, 67*, 87*, 69, 70, 65, 54, 73*, 56*, 73; R.S. Rogers, 54, 50, 81,88; C.A.V. Checkland, 58, 65; P.A. Sharman, 76, 59; A Springett, 61; and Alfd. Goodwin, 96. The feature of the season has been the fine all-round play of L. de Montezuma, who has been quite the mainstay of the club, having beaten all previous club records in his aggregate of 878 runs, and having the fine average of over 38 per innings; this has only once been before beaten in the annals of the club - viz, in 1889, when W. Austin's average was 70. He has also bowled well throughout the season, but without any luck, and, although he has obtained the most wickets, his average gives no proper criterion of the good service he has done with the leather.

Alfd. Goodwin, C.A. Checkland, A Springett, and R.S. Rogers have all batted consistently well, and have nearly always been good for double figures. Frank Hallam has been very disappointing this season, and it seems strange not to record his name amongst the scorers of 50 and upwards. W. Austin, except for his "century", did not bat up to his proper form. T.D. Lee also, who, when set, is one of the most dangerous bats in the club, never really did himself justice. We regret to say that Dr Conan Doyle, who, last season, was of such great service to the club, has fallen a victim to the allurement of golf, and has, therefore, to a great extent forsaken his old love. P.A. Sharman and R. Grace have done nearly all the scoring for the second eleven, but the chief feature in their matches has been the bowling of J.D. Gillespie, son of a former secretary of the club, who has obtained 32 wickets at a cost of under 8 runs per wicket - no mean performance for a schoolboy. We look for great things from him in future seasons.

In the bowling department, F.S. Hallam tops the averages, having bowled very well, and, we think, should have been put on oftener. The most successful bowler of the year is undoubtedly W.C. Elborough, who has obtained 62 wickets at a cost of just over 9 runs per wicket - a good performance for an old stager on the hard, run-getting wickets of 1893. W. Austin, A.P. Roe, and R.S. Rogers have also done good service with the leather. The special performances to be noted are W. Austin's 8 wickets for 23 runs v. Brixton Wanderers on 4th July, and 7 wickets for 15 v. Chislehurst on 22nd May; W.C Elborough's 7 for 11 v. Grecians, 22nd July, and 9 for 56 v. Kenley on 9th Sept;

Gillespie's 7 for 49 v. Forest Hill on 17th June; F. Hallam's 5 for 13 v. Carshalton on 6th May; and R. Rogers' 5 for 19 v. Grecians on 10th June.

The season has been all in favour of the batsmen, hence the number of drawn games, it being quite impossible for two strong sides to finish a match in an afternoon. The closure has been applied several times, but seldom with any definite result, and it has the objection of several members not getting an innings, and, therefore, not qualifying for the averages, notably F. Loud, who, although playing in 15 matches, has only batted nine times (ten being the qualifying number).

* Signifies not out.

Season, 1894

What with the bad weather and other unavoidable causes, the local club have not had such a successful season as in former years. Of the 37 matches played, the first eleven have won nine, lost seven, and drawn ten, and the second eleven have won two, lost five, and drawn four. The total number of runs scored for the club have been 4,866 for 298 wickets, or an average of 16.33 runs per wicket; whilst the opponents have scored 4,661 runs for 317 wickets, or an average of 14.70 runs per wicket. Three centuries have been scored for the club - viz., 113* by A.P. Roe, v. Northbrook; 101* by Alfred Goodwin, v, Spencer II; and 100 by Dr. Conan Doyle, v. Burlington Wanderers. Other scores of 50 and upwards have been as follows: - W. Austin, 68, 70, 62, 80; A. Conan Doyle, 64; Alfred Goodwin, 55; F.S. Hallam, 58*; T.D. Less, 72, 74; L. de Montezuma, 51, 60; A.P. Roe, 68*, 72*, 98; R.S. Rogers, 52.

The highest batting average has been deservedly obtained by A.P. Roe, who has batted very well throughout the season, has obtained the highest aggregate number of runs, and also comes second in the bowling averages, although the slow wickets have not been favourable to his bowling. W. Austin has also got back to his old form this season, and has played several fine innings.

The steady play of Dr. Conan Doyle has also been of incalculable service to the club on several occasions, and we much regret his intention of leaving the neighbourhood, as it will cause a serious loss to the cricket club. T.D. Lee and Alfred Goodwin gave the opponents a taste of their hitting powers on more than one occasion. L. de Montezuma, not being well at the early part of the season, was distinctly out of form for some time, and did not play as often for the club as in previous years. Frank Hallam batted in very good style, but with bad luck.

In the bowling department, R.S. Rogers comes well at the top of the list, his nine wickets for one run against Surbiton on the 30th June being not only a club, but a "cricket" record. Other good bowling performances were:- Roe's four for 13 against Carshalton; Hallam's six for 13 v. Carshalton; Elborough's six for 16 and six for nine v. London and Westminster Bank; Dr. A. Conan Doyle's six for 19 v. Northbrook, and five for 20 v. Crystal Palace. The club are fortunate in possessing a first-class wicket-keeper in F. Loud, but professional studies interfered with his playing so frequently as he otherwise would have done. His place, however, has been ably taken by T.D. Lee, C.A.V. Checkland, and G. Schuman.

* Signifies not out.

Appendix B - Selected Articles from *The Norwood News* 1891 - 1894

All of the articles that follow have been referred to earlier in this book.

MRS. BESANT'S LECTURE ON THEOSOPHY.

SIR,—The chairman of the meeting the other night was, I presume, within his right in limiting the speakers, who followed after the lecturer, to a bare five minutes. A debate, in which one of the speakers speaks for more than an hour, and the rest for five minutes a-piece, can scarcely be called a "Debate." But let that pass. Mrs. Besant's time was limited, and she was our guest with a preferential claim, for that night only, on our attentions. One consequence, however, was that, before I had fairly broken ground in my reply to her, I was interrupted and my remarks were brought prematurely to a close. May I then ask you kindly to insert the following brief summary of what I was proposing to say?

The opening part of Reverend John Rice Byrne's letter to The Norwood News which was published on October 31st 1891. It contains his criticism of A.C.R. Williams' handling of the debate.

One word more as to my responsibility for the "debates," as they are called, of the Upper Norwood Literary and Scientific Society. I am chairman of the society, and as such take my full share of responsibility for the arranging of what are termed the "lectures," and the appointing of the lecturers. Their names alone are a sufficient guarantee of their merits — the Rev. R. Haweis, Professor Gardiner, the Bishop of Ripon, Mrs. Fawcett, and Mr. H. G. Keene, with Mr. Brandram for a dramatic recitation. With the arranging of the "debates," their subjects, and who should open them, I have had nothing to do. That duty was assigned to a sub-committee, of which I was not a member. With three at least out of the four persons selected to open the debates I have no sort of sympathy. One is said to have been an occasion of infinite distress and misery to his fellows in the ranks of labour; another is a very great goose, but dangerous; a third is what she is.

Your obedient servant,

J. RICE BYRNE.

Closing part of the same letter in which Reverend Byrne disclaims responsibility for the society's debates.

MRS. BESANT ON THE REV. J. RICE BYRNE'S LETTER.

A member of the Upper Norwood Literary and Scientific Society, having sent Mr. Rice Byrne's letter to Mrs. Besant asking her if she would care to reply to it, has received the following letter :—

"DEAR SIR, —Thanks for paper (*Norwood News*). I do not think Mr. Rice Byrne's letter is worth answering ; it reminds me of nothing so much as a very angry kitten, with arched back and swollen tail, spitting furiously at a supposed foe.

With kind regards,

ANNIE BESANT."

Annie Besant's response to Reverend Rice Byrne's letter
(Published in Norwood News of November 7th 1891)

SIR,—After the severe castigation which the Rev. J. Rice Byrne received at the hands of Mrs. Besant the other evening, I was not surprised to see his very sore letter in yours of last week. He tells us he is not in sympathy with Mrs. Besant, who he describes as "What she is"—perhaps meant to be complimentary—and yet he attends the debate. He also attacks the chairman, who earned my life-long gratitude by stopping a speech of the rev. gentleman which might have been going on now, and which the audience certainly didn't want to hear. For the future I strongly advise, and certainly hope, that the Rev. J. R. Byrne will let us have our debates to ourselves, which I am certain will conduce to the happiness of all parties.

Yours faithfully,
ONE OF THE AUDIENCE.

Letter from the same issue of The Norwood News which praises A.C.R. Williams and criticises Reverend Rice Byrne

Norwood v. The Idlers (12 a side).—An interesting match was played on Wednesday last, in miserable weather, when Dr. Conan Doyle brought a team composed of literary and artistic contributors to the *Idler* magazine. Some good cricket was shown, notwithstanding that rain kept on all the afternoon. Amongst the visitors were A. H. Wood, who plays for Hampshire; B. A. Clarke, of Hornsey; and J. B. Hatt, of West of Scotland fame. J. R. Goold played a fine innings of 74 not out, going in first for Norwood and carrying his bat through the innings. We noticed that the popular author of "Three Men in a Boat" was officiating as scorer for the Idlers. Score:—

IDLERS.

A. H. Wood, b Scott	8
J. H. Doyle, c Lond, b Ellis ...	25
J. B. Hatt, b Goold	30
A. Conan Doyle, st Lond, b Featherstone	17
Eden Phillpott, b McCausland ...	9
E. W. Hooming, b Ellis	10
B. A. Clarke, not out	27
J. Barr, b McCausland	0
G. B. Burgin, b McCausland ...	2
H. E. Clarke, b McCausland ...	0
R. Grey, run out	5
C. K. Milburn, b McCausland ...	0
Extras	17
	150

NORWOOD.

J. R. Goold, not out	74
E. McCausland, c Wood, b Hatt...	14
P. C. Scott, b Hatt...	8
G. Featherstone, b Hatt ...	0
P. A. Sharman, st Wood, b A. C. Doyle	0
F. W. Wiltshire, b Hatt	13
S. Ellis, b A. C. Doyle	2
W. W. Duffitt, c B. A. Clarke, b Hatt...	8
G. H. Gordon, b A. C. Doyle ...	0
F. Lond, c Burgin, b A. C. Doyle	10
General Bedford, not out	0
Extras	8
(9 wkts.)	137

W. Russell did not bat.

Norwood News report of 1892 Idlers cricket match

This report demonstrates how lax newspapers could be when it came to spelling. E.W. Hooming is clearly E.W. Hornung, the author of the Raffles stories and Conan Doyle's future brother-in-law. Eden Phillpott is actually Eden Phillpotts the author of a number of books set in Dartmoor.

Moving on from issues of spelling, there are other interesting items in this report. J.H. Doyle is Conan Doyle's brother Innes and A.H. Wood is Alfred H. Wood who later became Conan Doyle's secretary[126].

On a final note, the issue of the *Croydon Guardian*, which also covered this event, stated that one of the onlookers was J. Zaugwill. This was actually Israel Zangwill, the author of *The Bachelors' Club*.

---

[126] These details are all confirmed in *Out of the Shadows* by Georgina Doyle.

UPPER NORWOOD.

THE LITERARY AND SCIENTIFIC SOCIETY. —A business meeting was held at the Welcome Hall, May 25th, to arrange the work of the society for 1893-94. Dr. Conan Doyle was re-elected as president; Messrs. Keen and Williams as vice-presidents; Mr. Buchanan secretary; Dr. Murray Thomson as treasurer; and Dr. Morgan, Mr. A. Cummings, and Mr. W. T. Harden were added to the committee. A sub-committee was appointed to arrange a list of lectures and all the necessary details, which were to be submitted on completion to the full committee for confirmation. The accounts of the society showed a credit balance of £31. The treasurer was instructed to send a cheque for £12 12s. to Dr. Campbell, in furtherance of his work at the College for the Blind.

May 1893 article from The Norwood News reporting Conan Doyle's re-election as president of the UNLSS

UPPER NORWOOD

Literary and Scientific Society.

Syllabus of Lectures

1893—94.

1893.

Oct. 4.—"SOME FACTS ABOUT FICTION." A. Conan Doyle, M.D.

„ 11.—"RECENT EVIDENCES AS TO MAN'S SURVIVAL OF DEATH.' F. W. W. Myers, M.A.

„ 25. —"TWENTY THOUSAND FEET ABOVE THE LEVEL OF THE SEA." Edward Whymper F.R.G.S., Author of "Scrambles Am·ngst the Alps"; "Travels Amongst the Great Andes of the Equator." Fully Illustrated by Photos and Sketches by the Lecturer, and shown by the Oxyhydrogen Light.

Nov. 8.—"ACROSS ASIA ON A BICYCLE." Thomas Stevens. Illustrated with over Sixty Graphic Scenes, Incidents, and Adventures of his Ride through Turkey, Persia, Afghanistan, India, China, and Japan.

„ 22.—"THE LOST CONTINENT; A MISSING CHAPTER IN THE GEOGRAPHICAL DISTRIBUTION OF BIRDS." R. Bowdler Sharpe, LL.D., F.L.S., F.Z.S. Illustrated by Slides specially prepared by J. G. Keulemans, the well-known Natural History Artist, shown by the Oxy-hydrogen Light.

The Norwood News article detailing the lectures to take place in 1893

1894.

JAN. 17.—"DANTE." PHILIP H. WICK-
STEED, M.A.

„ 31.—"MOROCCO." J. E. BUDGETT
MEAKIN (for many years Editor of
The Times of Morocco). The Lecture
is fully Illustrated with Lantern
Slides. The Lecturer will appear in
Native Costume. Mr. Budgett
Meakin has lived in Morocco for many
years, and as he has a complete knowledge of the language, his opportunities
for studying the people and country
have been unique.

FEB. 14.—"LIFE AND DEATH OF
WORLDS." Mrs. PROCTOR, Widow
of the late Professor R. A. Proctor.
Illustrated by Lantern Slides.

„ 28.—"CONSTANTINOPLE AS AN
HISTORICAL CITY." FREDERIC
HARRISON.

MAR. 14.—"MEN AND MANNERS OF
THE PARLIAMENT OF 1893."
F. CARRUTHERS GOULD, the well-
known Parliamentary Caricaturist.
The Lecture is strictly non-party, and
is very fully Illustrated by Portraits,
Caricatures, Views, &c., to be shown
by the Oxy-hydrogen Light.

„ 28.—"SHIFTS FOR A LIVING
AMONGST ANIMALS." J. ARTHUR
THOMSON, M.A., Lecturer on Zoology
and Biology in the School of Medicine,
Edinburgh; Joint Author with Pro-
fessor Geddes of the "Evolution of
the Sex" (Contemporary Science
Series); and Author of "The Study
of Animal Life, &c." (University
Extension Manuals).

*The Lectures will be held at the
Royal Normal College, at 8.15 p.m.*

Continuation of the same article showing the lectures for 1894

UPPER NORWOOD LITERARY AND SCIENTIFIC SOCIETY.

The annual meeting of the Upper Norwood Literary and Scientific Society, which marks the close of the season, was held on Friday evening, the 11th inst., at the Welcome, Westow-street. Dr. A. Conan Doyle occupied the chair, and there were present Mr. H. B. M. Buchanan (secretary), Mr. J. Judd, C.C., Mr. S. Bromhead, Mr. A. C. R. Williams, Mr. A. Cummings, Mr. Page, and Mr. W. G. Harrison.

Mr. S. BROMHEAD presented the balance-sheet on behalf of Dr. Murray Thompson, who was unable to be present. The balance over from last season was £15 12s. 6d. The receipts for the year amounted to £108 4s. 6d., and the expenditure was £103 0s. 0½d., which left a balance to carry to the next account of £5 4s. 5½d. There were nine lectures given, and £23 2s. figured as the cost of hiring the hall, which amount Dr. Campbell did not see his way to reduce.

The CHAIRMAN said he regretted exceedingly that he would have to vacate the presidential chair, for at least some years to come, as he intended spending the winters abroad. He thanked them for the kindness shown in placing him in that position, and assured them the time so spent would always be a very pleasant recollection.

Opening section of The Norwood News article of May 1894 that covered Conan Doyle's resignation from the UNLSS

Mr. JUDD moved that the resignation be received with great regret, for Dr. Conan Doyle had done most valuable service in promoting the prosperity of the society.

Mr. BROMHEAD seconded, and the motion was unanimously carried.

The CHAIRMAN—I thank you very much. It is very kind of you. Though I have to leave, I trust you will keep my name on the committee, so that at least I may have some little connection with the society. (Loud applause.)

Mr. BUCHANAN proposed Mr. C. E. Tritton, M.P., to take Mr. Doyle's place. He had promised to do so and attend as many of the meetings as he could.

Mr. JUDD seconded, and the motion was unanimously carried.

The CHAIRMAN said he thought Mr. Tritton would make a most excellent president. Concerning the secretaryship, Dr. Doyle said he was sure all would agree with him that no change was required, for Mr. Buchanan had worked most unselfishly in the interests of the society. (Hear, hear.) Its success was mainly due to his assiduous care and attention.

Mr. BUCHANAN said he would be glad to continue as heretofore.

Continuation of the same article covering some of the committee appointments

Bibliography

Baring-Gould, W.S. The Annotated Sherlock Holmes. ISBN 978-0517502914

Baring-Gould, W.S. Sherlock Holmes - A biography of the world's first consulting detective. Panther. ISBN 586-04260-1

Carr, John Dickson. The Life of Sir Arthur Conan Doyle. Carroll & Graff. ISBN 07867 1234 1

Doyle, Arthur Conan. Memories and Adventures. Wordsworth Editions Ltd. ISBN 978-1840225709.

Doyle, Arthur Conan. The Memoirs of Sherlock Holmes. Oxford World's Classics. ISBN 978-0192838117.

Doyle, Georgina. Out of the Shadows. Calabash Press. ISBN 1-55310-064-6

Foley, Charles. Stashower, Daniel. Lellenberg Jon. Arthur Conan Doyle - A Life in Letters. Harper Collins. ISBN 978-0-00-724759-2

Green, Richard Lancelyn. Conan Doyle of Wimpole Street. The Arthur Conan Doyle Society. ISBN 978-1899060023.

Green, Richard Lancelyn. Gibson, John. A Bibliography of A. Conan Doyle. Clarendon Press. ISBN 978-0198181903.

Lycett, Andrew. Conan Doyle - The Man Who Created Sherlock Holmes. Weidenfeld & Nicolson. ISBN 0297848526

Mannix, John Bernard. Heroes of the Darkness. S.W. Partridge.

Pearson, Hesketh. Conan Doyle. White Lion Publishers. ISBN 0 85617 377 0

Pugh, Brian. A Chronology of the life of Sir Arthur Conan Doyle. MX Publishing. ISBN 978-1904312550

Rosenberg, Samuel. Naked is the Best Disguise. Penguin Books Ltd. ISBN 978-140040302

Smith, Herbert Greenhough. What I Think - A Symposium on Books and other things by famous writers of today. George Newnes.

Stashower, Daniel, Teller of Tales. Penguin Books Ltd. ISBN 978-0140285741

Stavert, Geoffrey. A Study in Southsea. Milestone.

Tracy, Jack. Sherlock Holmes - The Published Apocrypha. Gaslight Publications. ISBN 0-93-446824-9

Waller, Philip J. Writers, Readers and Reputations. Oxford University Press. ISBN 978-0199541201

Index

Also from MX Publishing:

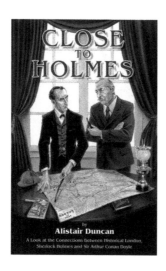

Alistair Duncan

Close To Holmes

A Look at the Connections Between Historical London, Sherlock Holmes and Sir Arthur Conan Doyle

Also from MX Publishing:

Alistair Duncan

Eliminate the Impossible

An Examination of the World of
Sherlock Holmes on Page and Screen

Also from MX Publishing:

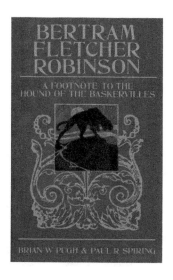

Brian W. Pugh and Paul R. Spiring

Bertram Fletcher Robinson

A Footnote to the Hound of the Baskervilles

Also from MX Publishing:

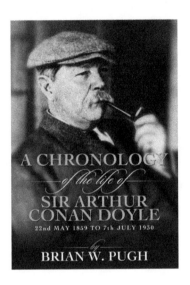

Brian W. Pugh

A Chronology of The Life Of Sir Arthur Conan Doyle

A Detailed Account Of The Life And Times Of The Creator Of Sherlock Holmes

Also from MX Publishing:

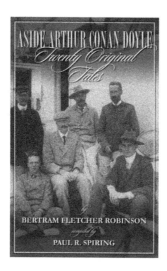

Paul R. Spiring

Aside Arthur Conan Doyle

Twenty Original Tales By Bertram Fletcher Robinson

CPSIA information can be obtained
at www.ICGtesting.com
Printed in the USA
LVHW05s0331170818
587263LV00008B/197/P